CAPTURING C. ____

Club Isola

Avery Gale

MENAGE AND MORE

Siren Publishing, Inc.
www.SirenPublishing.com

DEDICATION

To my crazy aunts who always encouraged me to speak my mind. Their wild and wacky senses of adventure helped launch my imagination.

CAPTURING CALLIE

Club Isola

AVERY GALE
Copyright © 2013

Chapter 1

Ian McGregor looked out over the still waters of the bay toward the shimmering lights of the mainland. Standing in front of the wall of windows in his bedroom suite gave him an amazing view of what he had always considered one of the most beautiful expanses of water on Earth. His many business pursuits required him to travel the world, so he figured his opinion was at the very least informed. Living on an island off the coast of his beloved Virginia had proven to be a dream come true. He valued his privacy and, considering his chosen lifestyle, staying out of the media spotlight was almost a requirement.

Even though he kept luxury penthouse suites in several cities, the home he'd built here was where he spent the majority of his time and where he felt the most comfortable. The entire structure was an eco-technological wonder. Hell, the patents alone on the energy-efficient building materials he'd designed for it would make him a billion dollars in the next ten years. And that was without adding in the software for the audio-visual and security systems. He had collaborated with his friend and colleague, Mitch Grayson, on several of the security system's features, and Ian was thrilled to be sharing the profits from those with Mitch. Sighing as he thought about how Mitch and his friend, Bryant Davis, had settled down with their wife and submissive, Rissa, he wondered if he'd ever be as happy as they seemed.

Glancing around the beautifully landscaped gardens between his home and the beach, he smiled, remembering all the time he'd spent listening to the Lamonts explain the "special" elements of the beautiful gardens behind The ShadowDance Club. He planned to implement some of their ideas behind Club Isola as soon as he figured out how to camouflage it from overhead. The members of ultraprivate Club Isola were, for the most part, very high-profile public figures, so media intrusion was always a concern. And while the patents for his island retreat were the moneymakers, it was the well-hidden building on the other side of the small expanse of land that had been his true motive for this labor of love.

Only a select few people had known about the deep caves on the tiny island, and that fact had enabled his purchase of the small treasure for well under its real value. The caves were deep and structurally sound with several natural outlets so ventilation and escape routes had been easy to implement. The island itself was just over two square miles in area and was long enough that he'd been able to add a small landing strip and helipad. The golf course had been designed by a member of the PGA who had traded his services for a lifetime membership to the club. As soon as he found the right manager, he wanted to build a small but very exclusive luxury resort he would simply call The Resort Isola.

While he'd been at ShadowDance Mountain last month, he'd vowed to lure away their newly hired motel manager, but Alex and Zach Lamont had threatened to castrate him if he did. He'd been in the room but out of her view during her interview and had been impressed with the Marilyn Monroe look-alike. Smiling to himself he remembered Alex growling at him, but it had been Zach's threat that had made him laugh and ultimately give up his taunts. Zach had threatened to sic their wife, Katarina, on him, and Ian was wise enough to avoid the tiny blonde's wrath. He'd also been smart enough to hire her on the spot to do his web-designing after he'd seen some of her work. He'd enjoyed teasing her about being too smart to be married to his Neanderthal friends. She hadn't missed a beat and had joined right in agreeing with him, something Ian was sure her sweet ass had paid for later that evening.

Looking down on to his private beach, Ian wondered if he'd ever share it with a woman who would appreciate it for all it had been designed to be. No one visiting the club or any of the island's other amenities would ever be able to get close enough to view the small strip of sand. The flora surrounding it was reminiscent of a rain forest, and he had even added a solar-powered waterfall cascading over eco-friendly and erosion-resistant material fashioned to look like the volcanic and granite bedrock found in the Shenandoah National Park. The entire area was so well protected there was rarely even as much as a white-cap atop the tiny inlet's water, and the white sand he'd brought in for the beach sparkled as if it was laced with diamonds each evening as the sun set.

Standing in the dark and thinking back over the past several years, Ian was surprised he didn't feel a deeper sense of satisfaction from all he'd accomplished. Monetarily the past five years had been more than he could have ever dreamed possible, but all the professional success in the world wasn't meeting the burning need in his soul. He hadn't even been able to pinpoint exactly what it was that he was looking for, so finding a solution in the near future didn't seem likely.

Just as he was ready to turn back into the room before heading down for a late dinner, something out on the water caught his eye. He'd just caught a distorted shadow in the glimmering lights that looked as if it had been about a quarter of a mile off-shore. Grabbing the night-vision scope he kept nearby, he stepped out on to the wide walkway that surrounded his private quarters and hit the small, hidden switch that suppressed the solar security and landscaping lights so he wouldn't be seen. As he zeroed in on the spot, he saw a shimmer of blonde. His eyes had to be playing tricks on him. Nobody would brave the frigid bay waters that far out knowing there was no way to avoid detection once they'd made their way on to the island. Mentally correcting himself, Ian knew that wasn't entirely true. There were two types of people who would try—corporate spies and reporters.

Ian had seen the company helicopter land about an hour ago, so he knew Jace would be in his office by now. He and Jace Garrett had been friends since college. After graduation, Ian had returned to take over his father's struggling business after his dad had died suddenly from a heart attack, and Jace had joined the Navy. They had stayed in contact even as Jace had gone on to become a SEAL. When Jace had decided to retire after a mission had gone so far south his friend had sworn to him he'd seen penguins, Ian had hired him as the Chief of Security for McGregor Holdings. Ian hit the button on his phone that would connect him directly with Jace, and Ian wasn't surprised when the other man answered on the second ring.

"Garrett. What's up, boss?" Jace's tone reflected his surprise. Ian rarely called him this late.

"Looks like we've got company. Meet me at the top of the stairs leading to the dock. Bring the night visions. I want to see who this is before we confront them."

"Roger that. ETA two minutes." Ian smiled to himself, nothing like the US Special Forces teams to drill clear and concise communication techniques into their members. But truth be told, Ian found himself using the same curt, cut-to-the-chase style in business as well, and he'd often wondered if it was Jace's influence or simply his own lack of motivation to listen to what was usually a bunch of dribble.

As luck would have it, Ian was already dressed in black jeans and boots. It hadn't taken him but a second to pull on a black hooded sweatshirt and grab a penlight. Moving quickly through his dark home and sliding stealthily out the French doors leading to the patio stairs down to the dock, he was surprised to see Jace already in place. *Two minutes my ass.* Donning the goggles, they moved silently down the stairs, staying to the side in the shadows of the trees. The cloud-covered moon would work to their advantage unless the intruders had night-vision optics as well, then it would be an even playing field.

Whoever the intruder was, he certainly wasn't a professional. They'd caught a glimpse of the interloper just as he'd landed unceremoniously on his ass on the dock's synthetic decking. The recycled material he'd used when building the small dock might be state of the art for durability, and it looked so much like naturally aged wood that most people couldn't tell the difference, but the stuff was noisy as hell. That had been a real sticking point and had sent the product back through McGregor Holdings' R & D department more than once. But at this moment, Ian was grateful he hadn't replaced the prototype with the much quieter third-generation product.

Watching as the trespasser scrambled around in a tangle of arms and legs, he and Jace had looked at each other in disbelief. Hell, the ruckus the joker was making would have been enough to attract attention even without the motion-sensing alarms that were no doubt lighting up Jace's office at this very moment. Ian watched as the guy fell not once, but three times trying to get his small boat tied securely and to unload his gear from the small dinghy.

Ian looked over at Jace just as the former soldier looked up at him grinning and just shook his head and chuckled. Just as Ian returned his gaze to the walkway, he noticed wisps of blonde wafting in the soft breeze. Those few escaped strands had obviously been what had attracted his attention earlier. He and Jace must have reached simultaneous conclusions, because just as he'd noticed the soft voice cursing a blue streak was definitely female, Jace gave him a quick but completely inappropriate hand sign for woman. Ian caught his snort of laughter just before it had broken free and managed to simply nod his agreement. The realization that they were dealing with a female prowler was definitely a mixed blessing. On one hand, restraining the tiny slip of a woman was going to be a piece of cake, but on the other hand, their usual methods of interrogation were going to need to be altered—significantly altered.

Chapter 2

Callie Reece would rather have eaten mustard-soaked sardines at every meal for six months than take this assignment. But her kid sister's tuition was due in just over a month, and Callie's editor had made it crystal clear that this assignment was *nonnegotiable.* Either she delivered the goods on the super exclusive sex club on the other end of this small island or she'd be out looking for work in the worst job market in over a decade.

Finding herself lost in those fears had been just enough distraction for the old "Calamity Callie" to rear her very unladylike head in a big way. Fracking fairy farts, she'd fallen down three times. Hell, she was going to be black and blue from head to toe at this rate. She was tired—no, she was exhausted. Lord love a leper, who knew rowing that small boat would be such hard work. She'd been aiming for an isolated beach not far from the other end of the island, putting her much closer to where she'd been told the entrance to Club Isola was located. But she'd run out of steam and the current had brought her to this small dock. She'd planned to hide the boat in the nearby trees and then make her way closer to the club before camping out until she could gather information tomorrow evening. She'd reasoned she'd be able to do all of this undetected and make her way back to the mainland without anyone being the wiser. But now that she hadn't been able to conceal the boat, she needed a Plan B, and she needed it ten minutes ago.

Patting her bag to make sure she hadn't lost her phone, she decided she'd just have to call her editor and have someone retrieve her weakling self when she'd gotten enough information to write the article that he'd so indelicately called her "Career Saver." Just as she reached the end of the walkway, she heard the soft rustle of fabric being moved against foliage just before she felt a hand that had to be made of steel grasp her upper arm. She let out a startled gasp a heartbeat before all her years of self-defense training kicked in, and she became the wildcat all her instructors had preached that she needed to become.

* * * *

As the head of security, Jace had been the one to step forward and wrap his hand around the small woman's arm. He'd known she was small, but he'd been shocked when his hand had completely encircled her bicep. And he'd been completely blindsided by her reaction. She hadn't screamed as he'd expected, she'd merely gasped a split second before she had gone completely warrior princess on him. Standing just over six and a half feet tall, he rarely had anyone, man or woman, challenge him, so he'd been shocked when the woman had actually landed a couple of decent blows before he'd corralled her.

Trying to salvage some of his dignity had quickly become a nonissue when he'd heard Ian's soft chuckle as he stepped forward to help secure the imp's wrists in a pair of flexi cuffs. Once they had the woman's hands immobilized behind her, he realized she was nearly as lethal with her legs, so he had simply wrapped his hands around her muscular calves and dropped her onto her ass while he waited for Ian to link several of the plastic zip-ties he'd brought along and secure them around her slender ankles. Standing her up he'd been shocked to discover she couldn't have been over five feet one inch tall and that counted the damned Catwoman boots she was sporting.

Swearing softly, he promised himself he was going to take that damned vacation Ian had been ragging on his ass about for the past six months. The day a ninety-pound pixie was able to push her elbow into his diaphragm was the day he needed to head back to the ranch and regroup.

* * * *

Ian had watched as Jace struggled with the tiny tigress. And he had struggled to not laugh out loud when he'd heard the large man's *oomph* as she'd landed a solid elbow jab to Jace's solar plexus. Hell, connecting a blow like that to a former SEAL was enough to earn her a point or two up the respect ladder. Grateful for the moon's reappearance, Ian stepped close and secured zip-ties around each of her slender ankles and then linked them together so that she'd still be able to walk taking small steps, but wouldn't be able to kick out at them or run. Surprised that she hadn't said a single word, he stepped forward and pulled the black knit cap from her head and nearly swallowed his tongue. The cascade of wavy blonde silk that fell around her shoulders before heading toward the top of her ass was the stuff of his every fantasy and wet dream. He couldn't wait to get the black smudge paint off her face because he was sure the little sprite was going to be a stunner.

Watching as Jace gathered her gear, Ian kept his hand on her elbow. When Jace turned back to them and nodded, Ian said, "Come, *Carlin.*" The minute he'd spoken the words she'd frozen and turned to him.

Ian watched the little warrior closely. Her face was bathed in the moonlight, and once again he wished she wasn't wearing that damned face paint because he was certain her skin would be luminous in this light. When she asked, "What does that mean?" he'd been surprised that a woman who had fought with such strength would have a voice that was a soft, airy siren's call.

Looking down at her, he answered, "It's an Irish girls' name and means 'little champion.' Now come along." They hadn't made it but a few steps along the path leading to his home when she stumbled again. Hell, what was with her anyway? She seemed to be the most uncoordinated woman he'd ever encountered—that is until she had started fighting and then she had been pure poetry in motion. Suddenly Ian realized his evening had just gotten a whole lot more interesting. Leaning down, he scooped her up into his arms. When she started to struggle, he simply squeezed her tightly to his chest and whispered, "Be still or I'll drop you." He was pleased when she settled immediately. *Hmmm—a submissive criminal? That would be a novel concept.* Suppressing the urge to laugh, Ian took the lead as they made their way back up the steep, carved rock steps leading to his home.

When they reached the back entrance, Jace stepped in front of him and tapped the code into the security system and then opened the door. "I'll secure these and meet you in your office in fifteen. That should give you time to get that crap off her face. We need to be able to see her while we sort this out." Then after glancing in her direction he returned his gaze to Ian before adding, "If I were you, I'd leave the little she-devil bound." With that he turned and stormed down the hall toward his own office and quarters.

Ian had already set her on her feet and watched as she winced at Jace's words and then turned back to him. When she looked up at him, he felt like he'd been hit by lightning. Her eyes were the most amazing shade of violet he'd ever seen. There was almost something mystical about their color, and he suddenly understood the fascination Russians had with tanzanite. Looking at her, he was immediately hit by the zing of sexual awareness that seemed to arc between them. He felt a connection that he'd only read about in the ancient folklore tales his father had always insisted he study. The elder McGregor had reminded his son repeatedly about the importance of honoring "the gift of his Irish heritage." Before this moment, Ian would have sworn the old romantic tales were nothing but pure fiction. But now? Now he had to wonder if his father hadn't been a lot wiser than Ian had ever known.

Taking her elbow firmly in hand, Ian led her to the small washroom off his office. Since he didn't trust her, he entered the small room also. He cut the zip-ties, then turned to her and simply said, "Strip." Watching as her eyes went wide and then dilated before they turned to ice, he had almost laughed when she tried to appear taller by standing on the balls of her feet. Jesus, the defiance was coming off her in waves, but there was an underlying sensuality that had been sparked to life. He'd seen it flicker in her eyes before she'd managed to effectively hide it. If he hadn't been a trained Dominant, he was sure he wouldn't have caught it, but it had been there, even if for only a millisecond. When she didn't make any move to comply with his order, he took one step forward and watched as she tried to step back but stopped when her ass came up against the countertop. "What is your name, *Carlin*?"

"It's...um...Callie. Callie Reece. Who are you? And why do you want me to strip?" Her voice had trembled in genuine fear, and while he didn't want her comfortable, he didn't want her so afraid of him that she completely shut down emotionally either. Hell, they'd never find out anything if she clammed up. Best she enjoy at least some of his attention, so he decided he'd give her a few options to consider.

"Well, Callie, my name is Ian McGregor and this is my home. As a matter of fact, I own the entire island you just tried to sneak onto. As to why you have to strip, I have to make sure you aren't armed, and I want that crap washed off your face. And since I don't trust you and I think you might well attempt to make a break for it, I'll be staying right here. Now, either you strip or I'll strip you. And if I do it, you'll get a paddling for my trouble, is that clear enough?" Ian knew he wasn't going to win any "Host of the Year" awards, but the tiny troublemaker was getting to him in a big way and he was losing patience with himself as well as with her continued deer-in-the-headlights stare.

Deciding to see how she'd react to his full-on Dom tone, he barked, "Now, Callie. Strip or suffer the consequences." Sceing the pulse at the base of her slender neck speed up as her breathing become more and more shallow, he was pleased to see her toe off her boots before unsnapping her jeans and lowering them before kicking them aside. When she slowly lifted her T-shirt over her head, he nearly came on the spot at the sight of her standing before him in a tiny black lace thong and front-closing bra. *God Almighty, the woman is an erotic dream come to life.* "Very pretty, but it all goes. When you have removed the last two pieces, spread your legs shoulder-width apart, and relax your arms at your sides. I'm not going to hurt you, pet, but I am going to make sure you don't have any weapons hidden…anywhere. And then you'll step into the shower so that I can see the beautiful woman I know is hiding beneath that black smudge."

Chapter 3

Callie was sure she was going to faint, she was starting to see tiny black spots in her vision, and she knew her breathing was too fast, but she couldn't seem to slow it down. She could hear the blood rushing through her ears, and it felt like her fingers were going numb. When he'd said he was going to check her for hidden weapons, her mind had flashed to all the old movies she'd watched as a teenager about women in jails and cavity searches, and she'd gotten so lost in those thoughts she had skated right over the edge of fear and into full-blown panic mode. In the back of her mind she heard him directing her to breathe with him and felt his hand splayed over her chest as his other arm held up. When she finally regained her focus, she realized he'd already removed her underwear and was moving her under the warm spray of the shower. Even though he was in the shower with her, he had left on his formfitting jeans and she watched in awe as they molded to him until there was little left to the imagination. *Holy crap! Did he have to be so damned gorgeous? And aroused? And well endowed? Geez, can't I at least catch a break once in a while?*

When she finally found her voice, she said, "I can do this...um, you are getting your jeans all wet." She had tried to move her gaze away from his growing erection, she really had—but she wasn't trying that hard, and she sure wasn't succeeding.

Callie was convinced she'd die of embarrassment and humiliation when he placed his fingers under her chin and lifted her face until her eyes met his. She could tell he was trying to not laugh, but his grin was still shining through and amusement clearly laced his voice when he chuckled. "Like what you see, pet?" She could only manage to nod her head.

A small part of her consciousness knew she was in way over her head, but the other ninety-nine percent was screaming, "Go ahead, jump in! The water's fine!" but damned if she was going to open her mouth and let that slide out. No, she was going to maintain her dignity, well, as much as a woman can retain after being busted trying to sneak on to a private island to spy on a sex club and then fainting at the thought of a cavity search while being naked in the shower with a super hot man she didn't know and then being caught hungrily staring at his cock—yeah, those were all dignity-preserving activities for sure! Giving herself a mental head slap, she took a deep breath and let it out slowly before saying, "Yeah, well, you are pretty amazing looking, for sure. But I think I better get myself together so we can get out of here. Um, do you have a robe or something I can wear until I can find my bag that your pal, Mr. Sunshine, confiscated?"

She was sure she heard him chuckle when she was reaching for the soap, but she decided to embrace the "ignorance is bliss" view and ignore it. After she'd scrubbed her face, she opened her eyes just in time to see his very fine and very naked ass leaving the small bathroom. She hadn't even heard him leave the shower so she was shocked to see that he'd taken all of their clothing with him when he'd left. Just as she finished up and was starting to dry off, he returned fully dressed and held out one of his shirts for her to wear. He handed it to her and when she started to ask about underwear he simply said, "No, this is all you will be given to wear for this discussion. And, Callie, you are to button the center two buttons only, do I make myself clear?"

She was startled, but his tone wasn't one she wanted to argue with, so she simply replied, "Yes, Sir," before quickly pulling the large shirt on and attempting to secure the middle buttons. She felt like she was drowning in the shirt and was actually relieved when he stepped forward to help her.

"Let me help you. Only the middle two buttons, and let's roll up the sleeves so you have use of your hands." And then as if he were actually talking more to himself than to her, he added, "Another day I'll use those long sleeves to my advantage, little one." When he looked into her eyes, she was surprised to see the dark depths of his midnight blue eyes full of heat. And when he stepped back from her, she almost felt as if she'd wilted. It was as if someone had drained the energy from her. She knew he watched as she leaned against the counter in an effort to steady herself, and she'd seen him suppress a smile when she muttered about him being surrounded by a force field all his own, and just being near him was enough to light her up on the inside. *Fuck a duck, I can't believe I said that out loud.* She saw him start to ask her what that meant, so she quickly ducked her head and went back to trying to finger comb the tangles from her long hair.

Ian moved to the doorway and just stood watching as the tiny pixie tried to get the tangles out of her silken tresses. He finally had enough, and then, retrieving a wide-tooth comb from the drawer, he encircled her delicate wrist with his hand and pulled her to a leather chair in front of his desk. Knowing the leather would be a shock to her bare ass, he chuckled softly at her surprised gasp. "Something wrong?" When she didn't answer, he wrapped his fist in her hair and slowly tilted her face until they were nearly nose-to-nose and darkened his tone to say, "When I ask you a question, pet, I expect you to answer me immediately and with complete honesty. Do you understand?"

"Y–yes, Sir, I mean, yes, Mr. McGregor." She might have stumbled over the words, but her need was clearly written in her expression. His initial impression had been dead on, the small woman was a true submissive, and he wondered if she even knew what a sub was. It was likely she was thoroughly confused about her reaction to him, and that was something he intended to use to his advantage. He planned to make the most of her unsettled state, using it to his benefit while he found out exactly what she was up to.

"Now, answer my question, pet. Is there something wrong with the chair I have chosen for you? Would you like to move to another?" He knew perfectly well she wouldn't want to expose her delicate ass cheeks to another cold chair, but he merely looked deep into her violet eyes and waited.

"No, this chair is fine. It was just, well, my tush was all warm, and when it hit the cool leather, well…it startled me a bit. But this chair is warm now, so I don't want to move." She had started out looking into his eyes, but being a true submissive her gaze had slowly tracked down until it was now locked on her delicate hands which were tightly clasped in her lap. By the time she'd finished speaking, all he could see was the top of her head. He would let her hide this once, but that was going to end—quickly.

He carefully worked the tangles from her hair and was just finishing when he heard his friend's knock at the door. Jace had entered immediately and walked to Ian's desk, placed a folder on top, then taken a seat in the chair beside Callie's. Ian saw his friend give her a sideways glance and then look back at him. If he hadn't known Jace so well, he might have missed the small upward tilt of his eyebrow and the twitch at the corners of the man's lips before his expression returned to stone-cold distant.

Making sure Callie felt vulnerable while they questioned her wasn't an accident, and Jace would have known immediately exactly what he'd intended when he'd dressed the little warrior in next to nothing. They were both Doms, and even though Ian knew that Jace played more on the edgy side, there were some traits that all Doms shared. Keeping a sub a bit unbalanced was always about the power play, and in this situation it was completely warranted.

Chapter 4

Ian reached forward, flipped open the folder, and quickly scanned the contents. Obviously she'd been telling the truth about her name. Well, at least she'd been close, but it was likely Miss Reece had given him her standard answer to that question. If his assessment was correct, the woman in front of him was probably not very skilled at deception. He had discovered years ago true submissives are almost always very poor liars. But the few he'd met that could lie had, almost without exception, been both very skilled and pathological. In most true subs, the need to please is so deeply ingrained in their psyche that they were willing to go to great lengths to avoid answering a question rather than lie, particularly if they had reason to think the answer was something their Dom didn't want to hear. But more often than not their body language would give them away long before a Dom had to push them for an answer.

Deciding to let their pint-sized prowler squirm a bit longer, he pretended to read all sorts of interesting things in her file, when in fact the only thing he found interesting was that she had been her younger sister's sole means of support for more than two years and that she had cut her own college career short to subsidize her younger sibling's education. She was obviously still supporting the young woman who claimed she was attending a small but well-respected university in southern Florida. The copies of Callie's bank statements showed regular transfers into her sister's account, the large checks written with notations that they were for books and tuition. *Claimed? What the fuck did that mean? Interesting.*

Callie had eventually finished her degree in hotel management via online classes, but had taken a much lower-paying position working for some ass hat who had sent her to spy on him. No doubt she had taken the first job that had come along to avoid any downtime in income. Jace Garrett's ability to gather intel in incredibly small increments of time had always impressed the hell out of Ian, and truthfully, he wasn't an easy man to impress.

As he read further he nearly laughed out loud when he saw who she worked for. Hell, that rag of a tabloid had been trying to get someone into his club for months. It had been a running joke among his staff members because it was obvious the small tabloid's staff wasn't aware of the fact that Ian owned their parent company. But, at least now he knew she wasn't trying to steal trade secrets. He took a few minutes to begin formulating a plan—one that he was sure would hold a great amount of appeal for the desperately financially challenged little reporter. He closed and then dropped the folder back on to his desk. Then he leaned further forward in his leather chair before steepling his fingers in front of him and just watched her. She was sitting across from him with her bare pussy snuggled against the leather chair he'd have to look at each day from now forward. Christ, he wouldn't get any damned work done with that chair flaunting its enviable experience in his face every day. He'd probably have to redecorate the fucking shower, too.

Under his watchful gaze, she started to squirm, and it was obvious the instant she became aware of the fact her pussy was creaming the leather beneath her and that the evidence of her arousal was going to be obvious as soon as she stood up.

He waited until he could see she was a breath away from taking a header into panic again before giving in and deciding to it was time to give her something else to think about. "So tell me, Callie, what did your employer use as leverage to get you to agree to spy on Club Isola?" In his peripheral vision, Ian saw Jace's chest tense as if he were holding his breath, no doubt his friend was trying desperately to not laugh out loud at the look on her face. *Hope you don't play poker, little sub, because every emotion writes itself all over your beautiful face.*

Ian could almost see Callie gathering herself up and preparing for battle. He was anxious to see if she'd try to lie to him. If she did, it would just give him more power over her, something she was going to learn a lot more about if he had his way. He just sat and waited as she seemed to be waging an internal battle. He didn't have any doubt that she was trying to determine how much she could truthfully reveal without giving away everything.

Leaning back in his chair, he just watched her and took stock of the exquisite woman sitting in front of him. Her hair wasn't just blonde, it was actually several different shades of blonde layered together. The more it dried, the lighter and wavier it became. He'd been fascinated by its texture when he'd combed it earlier and wondered what it would feel like spread over his thighs as she sucked him down. Knowing that the mass of silky waves reached her sweet ass meant that when walked beside her and placed his hand at the small of her back, he'd be able to entangle his fingers in the golden curtain of curls. Fuck, that thought alone sent blood rushing south in a big way. She was small, probably just barely five feet tall. Her features were as close to perfect as he'd ever seen, and he briefly wondered for just a minute why she hadn't been tagged by some ruthless ad agency whose agents wouldn't have batted an eye at exploiting her perfection for their financial gain.

While it was easy to get lost in her physical beauty, it was the core of her that attracted him the most. She was intriguing and appeared whip smart. He could see the intelligence dancing in her eyes as she watched him. She was trying to calculate the odds of coming out of this unscathed. Hell, it was almost fun to watch. Finally, she took a couple of steadying breaths, and then it looked like someone had let the air out of her. She sagged forward and said, "My kid sister's tuition is due in a month. My boss knows I need the money so he's holding this over my head. If I don't get this story, I'll be out of a job, my sister will be out of school, and I'll likely end up out of my *luxurious* studio apartment. And quite frankly, it's a real testament to how rotten my financial situation is that I should actually care about that place. Hell, I haven't had heat or air conditioning for two years. Most of the electrical outlets don't work, and the hot water heater died a week ago. The shower I took a few minutes ago was the first time I have been able to bathe in warm water in days because it takes forever to heat water on the stove for a bath. Gives you new respect for the pioneers, I tell ya. Have you ever tried to actually heat up enough water to warm a tub full of cold water? Well damn, of course you haven't. What the hell am I thinking? Well, I'm here to tell you it just is not possible. You can check it if you want to, but I wouldn't recommend it, your dangley parts would probably retreat so far you'd have to call in a search-and-rescue team." She looked up just as a single tear breached the edge of her eye and trailed down her cheek and he could tell she was shaken by the feelings of vulnerability her honesty had only served to highlight.

Dangley parts? What the fuck? Had she really just said that? Ian couldn't remember another time when he had wanted to laugh out loud during an interview with a submissive. When he looked up at Jace, he was surprised to see his friend's face was purple, literally. The ass was trying to hold his breath to keep from bursting out in hysterical laughter. Ian mentally shook his head. It would serve the prick right if he caused himself brain damage from oxygen deprivation. And speaking about missing out on a few doses of O_2— how the hell had she managed say all that without stopping to take a breath?

Then it was as if the spell of openness and exposure had been broken, and Callie seemed to pull herself together and, grasping her hands in her lap, she just looked at him for long seconds before adding, "You can check my story, hell, that file on your desk probably tells you everything but my shoe size anyway. I might not be the best investigative reporter, well, not the sneakiest anyway, but I'm honest, Mr. McGregor. I don't lie...ever."

Leaning back in his chair, Ian just waited. He had to give the little pixie credit, she was brave. And he didn't doubt that she was honest—at least with everyone but herself. But her sense of self-preservation certainly needed work. He doubted she'd use a safe word when she should, and that was something he'd have to correct very quickly. He'd always been a big believer in safe words, and they were *absolute law* at Club Isola. When he finally leaned toward her, he almost smiled when he saw her muscles tense and her eyes dilate. *Well, well, the little sub isn't as unaffected as she'd have me believe. How interesting—and convenient.*

"Let me tell you what I see, Callie. I see a beautiful woman who has taken on more responsibility than she should have to. I see a woman who honors her commitments, often at the expense of what she believes is right. I see a woman of integrity who prides herself on telling the truth to others, but who often lies to herself. I see an amazingly curious soul buried in the body of a very bright woman who struggles with her sexuality because she can't ever seem to get to the level of pleasure she is sure exists." He'd watched her eyes get wider with each statement he'd made and heard her gasp at the last one, so he knew he'd nailed it.

"Now, my question is—how brave are you, *Carlin*? Are you brave enough to seek that which eludes you? Do you want the story badly enough to explore your own desires?" God, he loved watching her eyes dilate even further with desire. She squirmed in her seat, and he knew she was trying to relieve the pressure of her swelling sex. He also knew exactly what she was *not* wearing under that shirt, so he'd be able to smell her arousal in a minute or two.

Chapter 5

Callie had nearly stroked out when Ian McGregor had started telling her what he "saw" in her. Pickle fudge, what was in that damned report anyway? How did he find out that much? No way in hell he could have just guessed so accurately. Now he'd thrown down a major challenge, and damn if that wasn't one of her biggest weaknesses. Damn it all to hell, she'd started getting in trouble with dares in kindergarten. Sure, she shouldn't have cut off that chunk of Julie's ponytail, but that stupid Joey kid had dared her, so what else could she do? No big surprise when she'd heard he'd wound up in prison. Served the little weasel right after he ratted her out. The bully had seen Callie's dad leaving the local bar and been all too happy to fill him in on her latest escapade.

She'd missed several days of school because she had been unable to sit down after her dad had used the buckle end of his belt to "teach her a lesson" or at least that was what he'd been screaming all the while he'd been lashing her. As usual, her mom hadn't been home. And when she'd seen Callie's battered body the next morning, she'd been more worried about her social standing than she had been about her five-year-old daughter. So, Callie had been forced to at stay home, pretending she'd been sick. She had hated lying, and she had steadfastly refused to ever do it again. Her dad had still beaten her, but he'd been a lot more careful to keep the bruises hidden when he'd realized she wouldn't lie for him.

Callie froze when she suddenly realized she'd been muttering out loud. *Christ, save me from myself! Could I possibly fuck this up any worse?* She looked up to see that Ian had moved out of his enormous leather chair and had knelt in front of her. He framed her face with his hands and used his thumbs to wipe away tears she hadn't even realized had trailed down her cheeks. Just as she took a breath to speak, Ian growled, "Don't you dare apologize, *Carlin*. I can't begin to tell you how sad it makes me that your childhood was so difficult. Know that 'punishment' is far different than 'beating' and alcohol has adverse effects on people's ability to make the distinction. But most importantly, I want you to remember, each and every experience— good and bad—makes us into the people we are today. You must be a very strong woman to have survived all of that. But, are you strong enough to challenge yourself? To seek what will fulfill you?" When he stood up, he brushed his hand lightly over her hair before returning to his seat. Looking up at her, he asked, "Are you ready to hear your options, pet?" *Oh, I had to poke the Universe by asking if things could get any worse, didn't I? I am so screwed.*

Callie stole a glance at the huge man sitting next to her only to see a look of compassion in his gaze she hadn't expected. Looking quickly back to Ian, she slowly nodded her head. "Okay, listen carefully. Option One is that we return you to the mainland and turn you over to the port authorities tomorrow morning. Since you had to cross the bay to get here, we'd contact the Coast Guard, and that is a different playing field, pet. You'd likely spend a couple weeks in jail before seeing a public defender thirty seconds before you appeared before a federal judge who might or might not release you until your trial, that is assuming you could come up with a minimum ten-thousand-dollar bond. Of course by then, your small apartment will have been stripped clean by the vultures in your neighborhood and your boss will have fired you and your sister will have been removed from her classes."

She didn't doubt any of what he'd just said was true, and the worst part was she had no one but herself to blame for the mess she was in. Sighing, she looked up at him and asked, "And what is Option Two?" *Honestly, it didn't matter. She wouldn't have a choice...not* really. She'd have to do whatever he said because she had painted herself in a proverbial corner. *Damn, why didn't I get a freaking boat with a motor?*

Callie wasn't completely clueless about the types of things that went on at Club Isola, she'd done her homework for this assignment after all. She wasn't going to even get into how many panty changes that research had entailed. Some of the things she'd seen online had frightened her, but most of it had ignited feelings she hadn't been able to get out of her mind, because try as she had, the images just wouldn't leave her head. She also knew The Club's name was a nod to his mother's Italian heritage and translated to The Island Club. What she didn't know is where the damn club was hidden, because she'd studied every aerial map she could find, and it just wasn't there.

Even with all her BDSM research, she had been totally unprepared for the complete metamorphosis she watched take place in Ian McGregor as soon as the question had crossed her lips. The man had gone from cavalier disinterest to focused predator in the time it took her to blink. She watched as eyes transitioned from casual disregard to lust-filled desire, and the effect was mesmerizing. She had never seen anyone with eyes as dark as his, there didn't seem to be any color to them at all. His dark skin tone and jet-black hair seemed at odds with what was certainly a very Irish-Scot-sounding last name.

Everything about him seemed to shift, he leaned forward with obvious intent, and his eyes flashed with arousal so obvious she felt herself draw back. "Option Two is that you belong to me for a month." When she started to protest, he stopped her by simply raising his hand. "You will stay here on the island. You will submit to me and do exactly as I command while you learn about all things BDSM. You will be given a period of free time each day to make notes, but you will not have internet or cell-phone access unless I am present. Club Isola caters to a very distinguished clientele, so you will not be allowed to have your camera, we fiercely protect our members' privacy. You'll get your story, *Carlin*, but I'll have the opportunity to approve and edit everything before the copy goes to print. You'll have the exclusive of a lifetime."

She could only stare at him, dumbfounded. When she finally managed to find her voice, she asked, "What about my sister? She can't wait that long for tuition money…and…well, why? Why would you want *me*? You are a great-looking, very wealthy from the looks of things, fellow. I'll bet women fall at your feet, literally, begging to be your submissive. I'm not anyone special, if you don't believe me ask my editor or my last boyfriend…although his current boyfriend might get pissy with you. See the last guy who was with me decided I was so frigid he liked guys better…so, why me?" Shit, she hated that she rambled on when she was flustered. She always said the stupidest things—not that they weren't all true, but still.

He leaned back in his chair and smiled. "It speaks highly of who you are as a person that your first concern is for your sister. I assure you, her tuition will not be a problem for you. I'd be interested to speak with your former boyfriend if he blamed you for your inability to climax by his hand. And if you think you are the reason he's chosen a male companion, you aren't nearly as bright as I'd thought you to be. And finally, I will answer your last question when the time is right. Now, do you know what hard and soft limits are, pet?"

"Well, I think so, but wait a minute here. What do you mean about Chrissy's tuition? I'm responsible for her. I can't just disappear for a month. She'll go crazy if I don't call her every week. She depends on me to help her out, I mean, I know she needs to be more responsible sometimes, but she'll get there…eventually…I hope. And, well, you didn't answer the other question. Oh fuck! You aren't planning to sell me or something are you? Oh damn, I have to get out of here." Callie felt her heart rate speeding up, and her breathing getting too shallow, but she couldn't seem to pull herself back from the edge. And damn it to hell she hated those dancing black dots crowing her vision again. And just as she tried to get to her feet everything went black.

* * * *

Ian was amazed that concern for her sister was Callie's primary challenge to spending a month with him, or at least it had been until she'd talked herself into the crazy notion that he was some white slave trader or some such insane thing. Jesus Christ, she'd gone into a complete panic and dropped like a fucking stone. Thank God she'd been within Jace's reach. If there was ever a woman who needed guidance and discipline, it was Callista Reece. *Oh, indeed, little one, I know your full name and that your shoes are a size six.* She'd been wrong about that, too—her shoe size *had been* in the report Jace had managed in less than fifteen minutes.

As Jace had transferred Callie into his arms, he'd given his friend a short list of calls to make. He would make sure Chrissy Reece's tuition was never a problem for Callie again. Jace smiled and said, "Did you look at the picture of Chrissy? Your sweet woman makes it seem as if Chrissy is a twenty-year-old struggling newbie to the college scene when that is not exactly the way I'd view it." When Ian shook his head, Jace flipped the file open and slid it closer to reveal a woman who looked like the polar opposite of Callie. Chrissy Reece had emerald-green eyes framed by long bangs. Her hair was the color of dark mocha and fell in a straight silk sheath to the middle of her back. But the kicker was that Callie's younger sister wasn't turning up on any college registry in Florida. Ian would also bet that Callie wasn't aware that Chrissy was, in fact, making a small fortune as a stripper. And while Callie had been living in poverty to help out her sister, the minx in Florida was enjoying all the perks of a two-bedroom luxury apartment complete with twice weekly maid service, twenty-four hour access to a health club to rival any Ian had ever seen, and a full-time doorman and other security measures. When Ian raised his eyebrow, Jace merely nodded.

"I want you here for the first two weeks, but then I want you to fly to Florida and make sure 'Cut Crystal' knows we'll be holding her accountable for every cent her sister has sent her, including interest. She should also know that as of this moment, the First National Bank of Callie is forever closed to her. We'll decide later what to do with her, in the meantime, get it all." He didn't have to elaborate. Jace Garrett knew he was to find out everything about both women. "Also, have her apartment packed up and everything shipped to the secured storage below the office. Send people you trust, have them send anything she might need here. If Daph goes, make sure she is well protected."

Daphne Craig had worked for Ian since the beginning, the second day after his college graduation, in fact. Her first year salary had been paid for by the Chairman of the Board of Directors for McGregor Holdings, Inc. and Ian had teased her ever since that she was the mouthiest gift he'd ever received. She was also the most valuable gift he'd ever received or at least had been until earlier this evening. His gut was telling him he'd have to rephrase that claim from now on.

"I'll make sure Callie is *assigned* to this story for the foreseeable future and make sure Daph gets her some different clothes—you wouldn't fucking believe what's in her bag. I want to paddle her sister's ass for taking Callie's money while she's been yucking it up in the lap of luxury. I had already sent two of our guys to secure her apartment, and the pictures they sent confirm everything she told you about the place, it's a dump but neat and remarkably clean. Tyler said it was the most amazing thing he'd ever seen." Jace shook his head before he pulled his phone from his pocket and showed Ian a couple of pictures.

When Callie started to stir in his arms, Ian nodded to the door and said, "I've got this, if you'd take care of the things we talked about I'd appreciate it. I have a punishment to administer, and then we'll need to feed her before putting her to bed. I can hear her stomach growling for Christ's sake." When he looked down into her sweet face, her eyes were open and she had the saddest expression it tore at his heart.

"Why the sad face, pet?"

"I am just so embarrassed...I have been working so hard to do everything right, and it just seems like the harder I try, the more disastrous things become. And you know I don't have any choice, not really. I have to do the second option, and I'm so afraid you'll send me to some horrible place and my sister won't ever know what happened to me and she'll get kicked out of her dorm, and I haven't seen her in so long and I don't have much in my little apartment, but it's all I have, you know? And I fell down all those times, and you saw that, I know you did, so now you know why the kids in high school called me Calamity Callie. And if I don't return that stupid boat on time, I lose my two-hundred-dollar deposit. And just look at my hair...I look like I stuck my finger in a light socket for Caesar's sake." By the time she'd taken a breath, Jace had turned and was striding down the hall, laughing out loud. Ian smiled and shook his head, hell, he couldn't remember the last time he'd heard Jace's full-belly laugh.

"Pet, first of all, I am not selling or otherwise getting rid of you. I fully intend to enjoy your company myself. That's not to say Jace will not be joining us regularly, but you will belong to me, make no mistake about that. Now, we'll be beginning your training tonight, right now as a matter of fact. Stand up. There you go. Now, look at me and tell me why you are going to be spanked, pet."

Watching as her surprise changed to arousal was one of the most interesting emotional plays of expression he'd ever seen. "Um, well...oh...hey! Did you say spanked?" Her attempt at outrage was nullified by the full dilation of her beautiful eyes. There was only the barest hint of their violet still visible.

"Indeed that is exactly what I said, and if you make me repeat the question, I'll double the strokes." He merely raised his eyebrow and waited.

"Oh…frack…probably because I tried to sneak on your island and spy on your club. But in my defense, I don't want to know about your members, only what kinds of things you are doing…well, I guess everybody really already pretty much knows about that stuff, so maybe Harry really did want to know who was attending your little kink parties, because he did say to take pictures that—Hey!" He'd cut off her latest spiel by pulling her over his lap and adjusting her to his liking so that her ass was nicely peaked and her feet weren't touching the ground.

"Enough. You will get extra swats for your earlier cursing, and yes, you are being spanked for sneaking on the island, but more important, you're being spanked because you don't take care of yourself, you live in a deplorably dangerous neighborhood, and I shudder to think when you last had a decent meal." He lifted the tail of his shirt up so that her ass was bare, and he landed the first three swats in quick succession.

He knew the intensity of the swats would surprise her, but she didn't cry out or fight him. "How many strokes you get will depend upon how well you behave during your punishment. Since this is new to you, you don't have to count, but you are not allowed to come without permission. Do you understand, pet?" When she didn't immediately answer him, he landed another three swats, these considerably harsher than the first three. "I asked you a question, Callista."

"Shit, you found that out did you? And I hadn't answered because I was trying to decide if you were joking about that not coming thing. And it's hard for me to think standing on my head…Sir."

He spanked her several more times before stopping to say, "Yes, I knew your full name from the moment I opened that file, and why you chose to lie about that is a discussion for another day. And no, I was not *joking* about not coming, and you'll understand that soon enough." He landed several more swats and noticed that she was pressing her legs together, no doubt trying to put pressure on her needy little clit. He was pleased to see she'd been lifting her ass to meet the strokes. Her ass had pinked up nicely, and now it was turning a lovely shade of crimson. He moved her legs apart and circled his fingers around the swollen lips of her labia. She was soaking wet with her arousal, and the smell of her sex was pure temptation. Just as he knew she was getting dangerously close to climax, he withdrew his fingers and resumed her paddling.

"Oh no you don't, pet. Don't you dare come until I give you my permission." He gave her another five swats before Jace returned. He'd heard her quiet sobbing, and then her hiccupped promises to not swear ever again in her whole "fucking life." He looked up at Jace and just shook his head. "Now, Master Jace has returned and—Damn it, hold still. I promise you, yours is not the first bare ass he's ever seen, although I'm not sure he's seen one quite this blistered for awhile. He's going to give you five swats for that little wildcat performance down on the dock and then we'll decide about that orgasm your sweet little pussy is begging for."

Jace stepped forward and gave Callie five quick but harsh swats. "Hopefully the next time I get my hands on your ass it's something a lot more enjoyable, Callie."

Just as Jace stepped away, Ian plunged his fingers into her wet cunt and leaned over her to whisper, "Come, my pet." Jace knew Callie's ass had to feel like it was on fire, and most of her babbling through her sobs was unintelligible, but he had managed to catch just enough to know she didn't understand how the pain had shifted to need.

He was going to enjoy teaching her all about that during the next month, if she lasted that long. And he was surprised how much he hoped that she did, because there was just something amazing about her. He couldn't have explained it if he'd tried, but she had reawakened needs in him that he had feared were long dead. His cock felt like it was going to burst, and after he had turned her back over so she was sitting on his lap, it had taken every bit of his self-control to not plunge into her depths and take his own relief. He felt her settle against him and fall asleep almost immediately.

Moving toward the media room, he nodded to Jace who opened the door and turned on the large television. After he'd found a music station with soft piano music, he turned on a few of the soft side lights so if she woke up before they returned, she wouldn't be frightened by the dark, unfamiliar room. Jace handed him a softly woven cover and said, "She is amazing. Do you think she knows?"

"That she's a natural submissive? I am sure she suspects. There's no doubt she would have done a good deal of research before attempting to do this story. So it's going to be interesting to see how many misinterpretations we have to correct. God, I hate those internet sites that are filled with wannabe Doms trying to lure unsuspecting women into abusive relationships on the pretense of dominance and submission."

As they left the room, Ian glanced back at the sleeping wonder that was Callie Reece. Her face was blotchy from crying, and her hair was a mass of wavy blonde chaos. She was so tiny and delicate he was worried she'd have horrible bruises not only from the numerous falls she had out on the deck, but they'd given her a pretty harsh spanking as well. But he had wanted to convey a serious message about her language and taking better care of herself. Growling that he was going to take a quick shower, he returned to his suite, leaving Jace to make them a quick snack.

When he returned, the television had been tuned to an action movie and Jace sat in his favorite recliner, sipping a bottle of beer. Ian nodded toward Callie in question, and Jace simply shook his head, letting him know she hadn't awakened. Ian sat on the edge of the sofa and just looked at her for long moments. She was so unbelievably beautiful she nearly stole his breath. Moving his fingers along the side of her face in a slow caress, he smiled when she pressed her cheek into his palm and sighed in contentment. He leaned down and spoke against her ear, "Come on, pet, wake up for your Master. I want you to eat something before I put you in my bed and sink into that sweet pussy of yours. I'm going to fuck you, Callie. Are you ready for that?" He felt her stir against him, and when he pulled back he was pleased to see her eyes wide open and locked on to his.

"Yes, I would like that very much, but, well, my ass still hurts." He had been so pleased at her agreement that he'd nearly missed the last part until he heard Jace snort with laughter.

"Fuck, Callie. You made beer come out my nose. That shit burns, you know?" Jace's words were tempered by his laughter, and Ian couldn't help but laugh as well.

"Well, pet, then I suggest you do your best to avoid future punishment spankings. And yes, before you ask, not all spankings are punishment. Erotic spankings will be for both our pleasure. And I assure you, you will love them." He pulled her into a sitting position and then pointed to the tray on the table in front of them. "Now, eat up, you're going to need some energy when we go to bed." When she took a small sandwich and started eating, he poured her a glass of wine. "Now, before we go any further, are you on birth control? And do you have a clear health report?"

His questions evidently surprised her, because she starting choking on the bite she'd taken, making him glad he'd already poured her wine. When he handed it to her, she promptly gulped it down, trying to ease the chokehold the bread seemed to have in her throat. "Mercy, give a girl a little warning before you cut to third-date questions, Mr. McGregor. You know, maybe you could hold up your hand with a number or something." Which she promptly demonstrated, using her slender hands to hold up three fingers. For just a second, Ian forgot about the sass and focused on her hand and the vision of how it was going to look wrapped around his cock.

She brought him out of his musings when she said, "I am on birth control, and I had a physical a couple of months ago, there should be a card in my wallet stating my health status. I haven't been with anyone since." Ian watched as her gaze dropped to her hands as she'd spoken the last sentence and was grateful she was so very easy to read.

Reaching for her, he caught her chin with his fingers and lifted it so that she was forced to look at him. "How long ago did you last have sex, pet?" He knew the answer wasn't something she would readily admit on her own, so best to just ask her straight out.

"Don't suppose you'd be willing to settle for 'quite awhile' would you?" she asked hopefully. Then she quickly added, more to herself than to him, he was quite sure, "Oh hell no, you're going to be like a dog with a bone on this one. I can just tell."

Ian was torn, one part of him wanted to upend her and swat her ass again for her insolence and another part of him wanted to hug her because she was so damned adorable. When she reached for the wine, Jace took her glass and refilled it for her, saying, "Best rephrase that, sugar, or you're going to get yourself another paddlin', and I'm not sure that sore ass of yours can take many more swats tonight." Callie had drained her wineglass by the time Jace had finished speaking, and he just raised his eyebrow at her in silent question.

Glancing down at her glass, she smiled guiltily and said, "Oh, sorry for that, but it seemed like...well, maybe if I kept myself busy...you know, drinking...I wouldn't be spouting off getting myself into trouble." This time, neither of them bothered to hide their amusement, and they both laughed out loud.

"Damn, boss, she is somethin' else. I think the next month is going to be mighty interesting. Hell, I'd been thinking about taking you up on that vacation plan, but I do believe I'll stick around now." Jace leaned forward and refilled her glass for the third time but cautioned her that it was the last she was getting before leaning back and grinning like a Cheshire cat.

When Ian just continued to watch her, she started to squirm before looking up at him through long, golden-tipped lashes and said, "Well, pickle-pops, you're not going to let this go, are you? Well, it's been seven years since I had sex. And I'll just save you the math and tell you, that puts it at the end of my junior year of high school." Ian noted that she had stopped eating, and her eyes had gone glassy and distant. He noticed her body language had shifted entirely inward, and even though he was tempted to let her have a bit of space, he knew he couldn't. He'd mentored Doms for years and had preached, "Begin as you intend to go," to each of them, so he knew he couldn't let her keep any secrets.

"Look at me, *Carlin*." When she finally raised her gaze to his, he hated the look of despair that he saw in her eyes. When he was sure that he'd gained her focus, he continued. "I know this isn't easy for you, and I know you would rather not share what I'm going to ask. But for the next month, I am your Dom, and as such, I won't allow any secrets between us, do you understand?" When she reluctantly nodded her head, he went on. "I intend to meet all of your needs, physical, social, financial, and sexual for the time we are together. As your Dom it is my right and privilege to do so. A sub entrusts herself to her Dom and honesty is the greatest part of that. Do you see where this is going? Now, it was written all over your lovely face that your experience was less than it should have been, and I want you to explain that to me so that I don't do anything that might remind you of that experience."

Ian watched Callie's eyes as she processed everything he'd just said. He'd known it would be easier for her to accept if he didn't just demand the information, even though he'd have been within his rights as her Dom to do so. But he also knew that her free-will submission would be far more valuable in the end than any small power play victory he could win right now. He suddenly had a far greater appreciation for his friends and club members who were in D/s relationships with women they loved. Because for the first time, he was struck by how much more challenging it had to be dealing with a sub you truly cared about.

Chapter 6

There wasn't much in her life she regretted more than not pressing charges against the two boys who had raped her that night. Of course, with their parents' money and influence nothing would have become of it, but she still regretted being such a coward. She'd let her mother convince her that silence was in her best interest. Somehow her social-climbing mother had turned the whole thing around until she was the victim and Callie was the selfish wench who had ruined everything for *her*.

Sometimes late at night she could still feel their hands groping her and tearing at her clothes. Their bodies, slick with the sweat of a hot summer's night, moving over her. The stench of stale beer on their breath as they'd forced their tongues in her mouth. The oppressive weight of them atop her as they forced themselves on her had been crushing. The bruises had faded within the week, but the emotional damage had been far deeper. And she had recently seen some very real progress in her war against those demons.

Callie hadn't even realized she was squeezing her hands closed until she felt the wineglass in her hand shatter, slicing into her palm. Ian had grabbed her wrist and was quickly pulling shards of glass from her bleeding hand while Jace had quickly started cleaning up the mess she'd made.

"Jesus Christ, Callie, didn't you just get your ass paddled for not taking care of yourself? *Carlin*, this is not the way to avoid another spanking. Come on. Up you go." Callie was registering the words, but they sounded so far away. She had been so lost in the memory she didn't realize Ian had scooped her up into his arms and headed down a long hallway until she heard him call over his shoulder to Jace to meet them in his bathroom with a med-kit. When she heard him say, "Make sure you have a magnifying glass and sutures," her head started spinning and she just laid her face against his chest and tried to concentrate on his heartbeat.

"Roger that," was the big man's only reply, and she heard his rapidly fading footsteps as he made his way down the hall in the opposite direction.

* * * *

Ian didn't have any idea what had happened to Callie, but it had to have been extremely traumatic to have caused what could only be termed a post-traumatic stress disorder episode. Ian had seen similar things happen to subs before, but usually there had been some kind of physical trigger. He'd never seen someone who appeared to be processing a request zone out so completely that they didn't respond to any verbal commands. He'd seen her gripping the glass with such strength he'd started shouting at her to release it before it shattered, but he hadn't been able to reach through whatever memory she'd been lost in. She hadn't opened her hand until the shards of glass had cut gashes into her delicate skin.

When Jace entered the bathroom with his med-kit, they set about removing each sliver of glass and washed the wounds thoroughly. Ian knew it had to have hurt, but Callie sat completely stock-still, never reacting to the pain in any way. Ian was starting to worry that they would have to call in professional help to get her to reengage when Jace spoke to him quietly. "I've got her. Why don't you go call Mitch Grayson? His gifts and experience with PTSD might provide some insight. Also, the man has access to information that God himself doesn't have the security clearance for—ask for his help."

Ian was reluctant to leave her, but knew they needed some outside help, and they damned well needed the name of whoever hurt her.

Leaning forward, he brushed his lips over her forehead and whispered, "I'll be right back, pet. Let Master Jace take care of you. Be a good girl, now."

She seemed to have heard him and met his gaze. Her eyes filled with unshed tears and she whispered, "I'm sorry." His heart nearly melted, and suddenly he wondered if he hadn't been wrong all these years. Maybe—just maybe he was capable of loving someone.

* * * *

Mitch Grayson had been a huge help and had promised to start looking into Callie's background immediately. Mitch had given him a brief rundown of possible triggers and explained how the men at ShadowDance had handled similar situations with their women. Ian had been grateful when Mitch let him speak with his wife, Rissa, because she had experienced enough trauma of her own to be a great source of information.

Before they'd ended their call, Mitch had promised to get back to Ian by tomorrow with the information and also suggested Ian make sure Callie was available so he could talk with her via video-cam. Ian remembered that Mitch's gifts as an empath were greatly enhanced if he could actually see and talk with the person he was reading. Mitch's ability to "hear" and often feel the emotions and thoughts of other people gave him unique opportunities to help people who had experiences they needed help resolving. It had also been an enormous asset to his SEAL team when they'd interviewed prisoners and victims alike.

They set up the call for 5:00 p.m. the next afternoon to ensure Mitch had plenty of time to gather information. Just before they signed off, Rissa asked to have the phone back, and Mitch had reluctantly agreed, and Ian had suppressed his laughter when he'd heard the very pregnant woman explain that talking on the phone was not a "taxing" physical activity.

"Ian, I just want to know if you are really interested in this woman? Because if you aren't, let someone else help her. It sounds like she has already had her trust violated in a big way, and well...adding a broken heart to her problems...that would just be mean...um, Sir." Ian laughed out loud at her words. It was easy to see why Mitch and Bryant had fallen in love with her. He thanked her for her words of wisdom and for looking out for Callie despite the fact they'd never met. It had been humbling when she'd quietly added, "Well, you know, I've been there and I know how hard it is...and I'd like to help someone else like Kat and Jenna helped me."

By the time he returned to the bathroom, Jace had sutured two of the deepest lacerations and gotten Callie changed into a clean shirt. Jace told him that he'd used topical anesthetic on her hand but didn't want to give her anything orally until she'd eaten. "Callie, tell Master Ian when you last ate." Jace was in Dom-mode, so Ian already knew he wasn't going to like the answer.

"Um...well, I didn't exactly say when, Master Jace." Her eyes darted between the two of them, and Ian felt his muscles tense. "What I said was that I didn't remember. That's not as bad...not really, because it could mean I just have a poor memory." Ian took a couple of deep breaths and counted to ten—twice. This was a real hot-point for him, and Jace knew it. When he crossed his arms over his chest and raised a brow, she quickly looked at the floor. "Okay, okay, don't have a stroke. I ate a package of ramen noodles for lunch yesterday. It's not payday yet and I...well, I'm out of money, okay?"

Ian was seeing red—literally. He wanted to put his fist through the wall because she was living in a hole-in-the wall apartment, in one of the worst neighborhoods in the city, with no heat or hot water, and she was not eating because she couldn't afford it while her sister was happily accepting help she didn't need. He wasn't prepared to tell Callie everything he knew about her "sister dearest" just yet, so he was going to have to temper his response.

"Come along, pet. We're going to get some decent food in you so you can take some pain medication, which you are no doubt going to need very soon. Then I'm going to start a tally of all the swats you have coming as soon as you are feeling a bit more settled." When he saw her apprehension, he gave her a mock glare before looking at Jace and asking, "Do we have any poster board? Perhaps some of that butcher's paper that comes on a long roll? I have a feeling I'm going to need a large piece of paper for this tally." Her giggle was probably the most beautiful sound he'd ever heard, and he was glad his words had hit their mark and lightened the mood a bit.

Chapter 7

Callie had been relieved when Ian and Jace had backed away from their previously *intense* moods. Ian had seemed to relax more and more with each bite she'd eaten, and truthfully, she'd eaten more than she'd wanted just because it had seemed to make him so happy. They had denied her any more wine, citing the medication they intended to give her, but she knew they were worried she'd have another meltdown as well. *Jesus, Joseph, and Mary, I know better than to drink. It always sends me ass over teakettle. I'm going to have to keep my wits about me if I'm going to get this story and survive this next month with my heart intact.*

As soon as she had eaten, Jace stepped forward and handed her a small glass of juice and a couple of painkillers, and she didn't hesitate to down them both because her hand was really starting to throb. It was only after she'd swallowed the pills that she'd noticed both men facing her with stern expressions. "What?"

Jace surprised her by pulling her roughly to her feet and then giving her a sharp slap on the ass. "Watch your tone, sweetness. You are already racking up more punishment points than you can pay off comfortably in a month. Personally I think Master Ian should renegotiate and keep you until you are even up—hell, he'd get to keep you forever. Now, why on earth would you take two pills from a man you barely know without so much as even inquiring as to what they contained?"

Callie was surprised by his suddenly stern demeanor and stuttered her answer. "Well, I mean, you said you were going to give me a painkiller, right? That's what I took, right? That was like Tylenol or something, wasn't it? Oh, fuck me, please tell…Hey! What was that for?"

Jace was grateful Ian stood back and let him play this one out with her. If he was going to have any real credibility with Callie as a Dom, he needed to start establishing that position of power now. Otherwise, she would always see him as a friend, even though he was actually the stricter of the two of them. If she wanted gentle and sweet, she'd trespassed on the wrong island. "You language is deplorable, sweetness. Clean it up or suffer the consequences. Now, you can, in fact, always trust what you take from our hands, but you had damned well always ask about what you are being given, even from us. It's called *informed consent*, and it's one of the tenets of BDSM that we live by."

What he hadn't told her was that his younger sister had always been deathly allergic to penicillin, and on a ranch that was something that had to be watched closely. Hell, she'd almost died as a young teen when she'd helped treat sick calves and inadvertently gotten some of the vaccine on her bare skin. Jace had just happened to see her staggering across the yard before she collapsed or they would have never gotten her to the hospital in time. And you could damned well bet nobody gave Abby Garrett any medicine without her knowing exactly what you were holding out to her.

"Oh, well, I guess you do have a valid point. I can see where that wasn't very smart on my part." *And why on earth I seem to instinctively trust you I have no idea, because I haven't trusted any man for many years.*

Jace watched as the emotions played out over her face, and when she finally settled, he saw Ian's slight nod, so he knew it was time to begin. They had wanted the Tylenol to kick in but not so much that her judgment was impaired before they began again. Looking down into her elfin face, he crossed his arms over his chest and said, "Strip, sweetness."

He saw her sharp intake of breath and then saw her eyes flicker briefly to Ian as if seeking his approval. *Oh, you do understand exactly who you belong to, don't you, angel. He already owns your body—he just has to get your heart on board. But I know something neither of you knows, you already own him as well.* When she hadn't removed the shirt quickly enough, Jace stepped forward and ripped open the garment he'd dressed her in not an hour earlier. "Holy shit…zus. You ripped Mr. McGregor's shirt. I'm not paying for that, you know. That was probably an expensive shirt…I can't buy expensive stuff that is good, let alone something that's ripped. Good grief, Gerty!"

Smack, Jace brought his hand down on her other ass cheek with a resounding crack. "Stop talking. And adding to the end of shit to make us think you're talking about puppies isn't going to cut it, sweetness. That's another mark on the tally." Turning to Ian he chuckled. "You were right about needing a long sheet of paper. Hell, we may have to devise a spanking bench/porta potty, she's gonna be on the things so damned long."

"Indeed she is, but I have to say, I do like hearing the sound of our hands coming down on her beautiful ass. And once we get her eating like she should, that lovely derrière is going to be a nice couple of handfuls. Now, present her to me."

Jace pulled the tattered garment from her body and tossed it aside before turning her so that she was facing Ian. He showed her how to kneel properly with her knees spread wide apart, her hands clasped behind her back, and her gaze lowered to the floor. "This will be the position you will take the most often, so it needs to be the first one you practice and become familiar with so that it is natural and comfortable for you. Now, when your Master tells you to kneel, this will be your position, understand? You'll be learning more as we go along." Then he stepped back so that he and Ian were shoulder to shoulder. Jace knew they were imposing when they both stood with their feet shoulder width apart and their arms crossed over bare chests, and it was always a good way to begin a scene—it put subs in the right frame of mind very quickly. But when Ian ordered Callie to look at them, Jace was surprised to see nothing but desire in her eyes. Ian had found himself a real gem—now if he didn't let his fucked-up past ruin it.

* * * *

Ian had watched the scene play out between Callie and Jace. He'd seen the horror on her face when Jace had ripped the shirt she was wearing, but he'd been shocked that it wasn't about being bared to them in such a brutish manner. No, her shock was because she feared being forced to replace an expensive linen shirt. The woman was such a natural submissive Ian wasn't surprised that those she loved could take easy advantage of her. If she were his permanently, he'd teach her that she only fully submitted to one man. Oh, he'd make her show the proper respect to other Doms, but *nobody* would fuck her unless he was in the room and gave his express permission. Jace would be allowed to play with her, but even his best friend wouldn't take his pleasure from her without Ian present.

"You have a lovely body, pet. You are a bit too thin, but we'll remedy that soon enough. I love seeing our pussy all bare, but tell me, how do you afford the luxury of waxing?" Ian was thrilled she was baby smooth, but he wanted to know how she afforded the costly treatments.

"Well…oh geez, this is going to sound awful, but it really isn't. You see, when I was in college…well, I sort of had this side business where I helped other students with their homework and stuff. I know I shouldn't have done it, but I really needed the money to help Chrissy because our mom had moved to California and wasn't established yet so Chrissy's care had sort of fallen to me. Anyway, a couple of the girls that I'd…um…helped quite a bit couldn't pay me, but they worked at a local spa, so they arranged for me to get free laser treatments." Ian shook his head in wonder. The woman was a constant source of surprise. And if he wasn't missing his guess, she probably had a wicked sense of humor when she was relaxed and alone with her friends.

"Well, bartering is an acceptable method of payment to be sure. And what you did in college to make money is history, pet. But I must say, I am pleased to know your beautiful pussy will always be naked to my eye. Now, stand up." He watched as she rose with a dancer's natural grace to a standing position before he continued. "Move your feet just a bit more than shoulder width apart and lace your fingers behind your head. That's it, perfect. I want to inspect what belongs to me for the next month. Master Jace is going to help me, and you'll allow his touch the same as you'll allow mine. Do you understand?"

"Yes, you want to look at me, to see if I pass your inspection." The quiver in Callie's voice betrayed her brave words.

"Close, but not exactly right, and I'll remind you that snarky responses will be dealt with harshly. And we'll be adding that one to the growing list of infractions you're going to be paying for later. Inspection can be for a number of reasons, but right now we'll be making ourselves familiar with your body because we need to know if you have any scars or skin conditions that we'd need to be careful of, we also need to make note of any bruising, etc. There are any number of reasons a Dom would inspect his sub, but the most common is simply because he *can*. Remember a submissive's body is not his or her own, it belongs wholly to his or her Master or Mistress."

Ian walked around Callie slowly, trailing his fingers in random patterns over her beautiful skin. Her skin was flawless, save the bruises that were rapidly forming on her ass cheeks. He saw her flinch when he pressed his fingers into the darkest of the bruises. "See, pet, this is exactly why it important for your Master to inspect your body. This bruising is more than I'd like to see, and it tells me that your body marks easily. I want you to feel a punishment for several hours after it's been administered so that it reinforces the lesson. What I don't want is to damage tender tissues, so this is something that Master Jace and I will take into consideration. But don't think for a minute there aren't a number of ways to *punish* a sub who is out of line that don't involve spanking, paddling, caning, or whipping."

Jesus, she was so responsive it made him want her all the more. Leaning over her shoulder, he ran his tongue around the rim of her delicate ear. "Remember, my lovely *Carlin*, a Dom's first obligation is to take care of his sub. I want you to be healthy and happy while I challenge you every single day to expand your horizons." Continuing to encircle her ear with his tongue, he suddenly plunged his tongue into her ear in several quick stabs, imitating what he planned to do to her pussy. "Are you wet for me?"

Callie's breath was coming in short pants, but she answered immediately, "Yes...I...I need...oh..."

"Tell me, pet. What do you need?" Ian wanted her to start saying the words he knew were going to be difficult for her to speak. No doubt she didn't speak that bluntly in everyday language—well, except for her very creative cursing, and he wanted to start blowing through those inhibitions immediately. "Say the words, sweet Callie, and perhaps Master Jace and I will give you what your body craves."

Ian and Jace had been steadily walking her towards the master suite, and he'd bet she had no idea they were even moving. Jace stepped forward and showed her the small butt plug he was holding. "Do you know what this is, sweetness?" When her eyes went wide, he smiled. "Judging by your reaction, I'd say that you do. Now, do you know why we might be planning to start you on the smallest of these now?" When she shook her head from side to side, he said, "That's not good enough for scene play, Callie. You'll have to speak the words so we'll always know you understand exactly what we've asked you."

"No, I don't know why it's important to shove anything up my ass....um, Sir." Jace watched as she lowered her eyes immediately, so she either knew her tone was a problem or she was lying about knowing why they were going to use the plug on her. Either way, she was being a brat, and it was time to stop that shit right now.

Jace's aim was spot on—without preamble, he pinched her pulsing clit between his thumb and finger. When she screamed and tried to push his hand away, he just chuckled. "Watch your tone or you'll find yourself bent over right here in the hall and this plug up your sweet ass without the benefit of preparation or lube. And I'm betting you know exactly what we have planned for you and why we're going to start stretching that sweet ass of yours."

They had reached the door, and Ian pulled Callie around so that she was facing him. "Go lie over the edge of the bed and spread your legs as wide as you can." He watched as she slowly made her way to the edge of the bed. When she'd done as he asked, he said, "Now, turn your feet in just a bit. Good girl." He'd walked up to her and stroked over the bruises that were becoming more prominent and frowned. "We really will have to be careful with you, pet. I don't like seeing marks are your beautiful skin for this long. And I particularly hate knowing they are going to be worse tomorrow. When you awaken in the morning, if neither Master Jace nor I are not in the room, remember, you may shower, etc. Then you will wear only what we lay out for you. Then you need to come find us so we can reassess this bruising. Are we clear on this, pet?"

"Yes, I understand." Ian could hear the airy quality of her voice, he loved that sound in a sub, it meant she was in the right mind-set for the rest of the scene.

"Now, my sweet sub, I'm going to watch as Master Jace works his magic on your sweet ass. You be a good girl and do exactly as he commands, and we're going to make you feel very, very good." With those words, Ian stepped to the side where he could monitor her reactions. He knew they were tossing her into the deep end of the pool, but she'd had a pretty stressful day, and quite honestly, he'd never found anything better at relieving stress than three or four "explode in your brain" orgasms.

Chapter 8

Any initial embarrassment Callie had felt when Jace had first shredded the shirt she'd been wearing was long since gone. Those feelings of hesitance had been replaced by a burning desire that was pulsing through her entire body. She would have sworn at that moment she could actually feel her heart beating by the way her clit felt as it throbbed with the blood that had rushed into the tiny bundle of nerves. She saw Ian standing to the side, and she could feel his gaze on her as Jace stepped up behind her and began massaging her ass cheeks. When she winced as he pressed into a particularly tender spot, her heart warmed when she felt him bend and brush light kisses over the spots that were bothering her the most. She knew that she bruised easily and could well imagine just how colorful she was becoming.

He spoke quietly against her skin. "I hate these marks. We have to find another way to correct her. And you, sweetness, simply must behave, because I don't even want to think about what a crop or strap or paddle would do to you." Sighing before he continued, she felt herself relaxing into his caring touch. She wasn't sure if it was the pain medication kicking in or the wonderful feel of his hands moving over her skin, but she felt as if she was being transported into another plane. She didn't usually take any pain medications because she didn't tolerate some of them very well. But she usually did fine with the milder, over-the-counter versions. *God, I am such a loser, just a little bit of attention and I'm floating off into space.*

She felt Jace's soft laughter. "No, sweetness, you are not a loser. And this is no ordinary touch. This is a centuries-old tantric method of massage that is meant to elicit exactly the responses you are exhibiting. And by the way, I love it when you think out loud, it makes our job so much easier."

It was official…Callie had sunk to a new low. She was going to die of embarrassment, and no one would ever know what happened to her. Her ass hat boss would deny ever sending her anywhere, Ian and Jace would be able to chop up her body and feed her to the fish, and that would be the end of it. How oh how did she get herself in these messes?

Coming back to the moment, she felt the slick lube just before Jace pushed his finger inside her rear hole. And she shuddered with a need that seemed to ripple through her entire body. "I don't know where you went for a few seconds, Callie. But I knew exactly how to bring you back, didn't I, sweetness? Push back against my finger as if you were trying to push me out. There you go. Now, just relax and let me take you for a ride. I'm going to light you up, babe."

She knew he was right the instant he started pumping his large finger in and out of her ass, gaining ground each timed he pushed back in. She felt electricity racing around the inside ring of her anus. She'd had no idea there were so many nerve endings there. She'd read about anal play and sex during her research, and it had intrigued her, but she hadn't had any idea it would feel this amazing. She felt herself pushing back to meet his fingers, and she knew the whimpers she heard were coming from her own lips, but she couldn't seem to control them. "Oh God, it feels so wonderful, not like anything I'd ever imagined. I really…oh, I really like it. But, I need, I need more…"

For just a brief moment Callie wondered why she wasn't afraid of these two men. She knew she had finally begun healing, but this was different from anything she'd ever felt. But instead of running in terror, she was absorbing everything she could, and it felt as if she had finally stepped out of the shadows into the sun.

She felt Jace lean forward and brush kisses over her shoulder blades just as she felt him insert two fingers and begin scissoring them back and forth. Her knees were going to go out from under her, and she was grateful he'd wrapped his arm around her so she wouldn't slide off the bed. And just as she thought it couldn't get any better, she felt him withdraw his fingers and replace them with the plug. He pushed it in steadily, and she felt her breath hitch, and just a split second before she felt it fully seat inside her, he pinched her clit and said, "Come for me, sweetness. Let me hear your pleasure."

Callie felt her body buck beneath him as a wildfire of desire raced over her. She heard herself scream her release and heard Ian growl from where he stood. "Fucking beautiful. She is so fucking perfect. Get her into position, I have to fuck her, *now!*"

She knew her body hadn't even completely settled from the mind-blowing orgasm Jace had given her when he lifted her and settled her in the middle of the massive bed. Immediately Ian was lowering himself over her, and she felt his cock probing her slick folds. "You are amazing, *Carlin.* Watching your beautiful release has made me desperate to fuck you. This is not going to be gentle, I want you too much. I want you to thank Master Jace for the pleasure he has given you by sucking his cock. When he gifts you with his cum, you'll swallow it all. Are you ready for your Master's cock, my beautiful sub?"

Before she could answer, he'd slid in all the way, and her tender tissues felt like they were burning and tearing as they stretched to accommodate his thick cock. The plug in her ass wasn't huge, but it was taking up valuable space, and just as she opened her mouth to scream, Jace pushed his rock-hard cock into her mouth. She immediately closed her lips around his girth and began sucking and swirling her tongue around smooth skin covering the head, relishing the taste of him and the feel of each vessel and ridge along his shaft. He slowing began fucking her mouth in a rhythm that matched the pace Ian had set between her legs. She felt herself racing toward release and wondered for just an instant if it was possible to die from pleasure overload just as she heard Ian shout, "Now!" and her entire world erupted into fountains of glittering colors that she didn't even know existed. She felt Jace's cock grow in her mouth just before she felt his hot seed pulsing to the back of her throat. She struggled to swallow each drop of the liquid that tasted both salty and sweet on her tongue.

She felt Ian's entire body shake and then felt his cock shooting hot seed against her cervix. She was still lost in the swirls of color dancing through her brain as Jace pulled his spent cock from her mouth and Ian lowered himself on top of her, as they all took deep, drawing breaths trying to slow their pounding hearts and draw much-needed oxygen into their lungs.

Ian finally rolled to his side, taking her with him, and she felt him pull her leg over his hip and hold it firmly as Jace gently removed the plug from her ass. She hadn't realized Jace had left the bed until he returned with a warm washcloth and set about cleaning her. When she tried to pull away in embarrassment, she felt Ian's arms tighten around her like steel bands. "Be still and let him care for you. Remember, it is our right and privilege as Doms to take care of you." And then he laughed softly. "And thank God one of us has enough energy left to do it. *Carlin*, I don't know when I have come so hard I couldn't even move afterward. You are amazing, my pet."

Somehow, they managed to get her tucked into the bed, and when she settled against Ian's chest, she heard the door click closed as Jace left the room. "Sleep, my sweet *Carlin*. You need your rest because I intend to wake you in a bit and make sweet love to you again…and then probably again, long before you will want me to. But you will submit your body to me, won't you, pet? And I'll enjoy the feel of the hot velvet walls of your pussy hugging my cock again and again." His fingers danced over her highly sensitized skin, and she felt chill bumps race up her spine and down each of her limbs. With her head resting on Ian's lightly tanned chest, she let the sound of his heartbeat lull her into a blissful sleep.

* * * *

As Jace Garrett walked back to his office, he thought back on his time with Ian and Callie and smiled. Damn, the woman was as naturally submissive as any he'd ever met and as sweet as they came. He could easily see why Ian was falling for her. Whether or not his friend would admit he was falling fast and hard was another matter. There was something very special about Callie Reece, and he was going to enjoy helping Ian train her in the lifestyle. He didn't see his role as anything other than a "third" for them, and that was fine by him. While he certainly liked Callie a lot, the spark that would be necessary to make a lifetime commitment to a woman just wasn't there. He figured he would always see her as a sort of little sister—but *not*.

Chapter 9

After he'd spoken with Ian McGregor and Jace Garrett last evening, Mitch Grayson had stayed up well into the night making calls and setting up numerous search programs. When he'd gotten back to his office at ShadowDance this morning, he hadn't been at all impressed with what he'd learned. And after making a few calls late this morning, he'd been pissed as hell. He'd called Ian at the agreed upon time and began relaying what he'd discovered.

"I don't have much good to report, I'm sorry to say. But I'm going to tell it to you straight and fast because I don't want your girl walking in during this conversation. Callie Reece was reportedly raped at a river party at the end of her junior year of high school. According to friends of her sister, she was sent to finish high school with an aunt and uncle in Kansas. And they are the only reason Callie was able to attend college. Worse yet, it seems Callie's mother blamed her daughter for her diminished social standing, which of course she claimed was a result of the rumors circulating about the 'alleged' rape."

In Mitch's opinion, the younger sister had obviously inherited the mother's gift for selling tickets on the Guilt Express because Callie had been sending her younger sister money for several years. Mitch had dug a little deeper after Jace had let him know "Cut Crystal's" career of choice and hadn't learned anything encouraging.

"From what I've been able to find out, Callie's father had been a moderately successful businessman, but his wife's champagne tastes and her habit of bedding any man *or woman* she thought would boost her social 'rank' eventually eroded his business, and less than a month after his business's collapse, Frank Reece was found dead behind their home. Local law enforcement termed the death 'suspicious' but his wife was able to collect her husband's life-insurance money and quickly relocated to southern California. She remarried a very wealthy, much older man within six months."

Taking a deep breath, Mitch continued, "Now, here's where it gets 'dicey.' The two young men accused of the rape were both from very prominent families, so information is hard to come by. But it seems Chrissy got sloppy drunk a few months back and started talking to some of her friends at the strip club where she works. She told them how her mom had demanded money from both families to 'deal with a pregnancy' that had never been and that Callie had never received any of the money or even known what their mom had done."

Mitch could tell that Ian was seeing red already, and he knew his friend was going to like the rest of the story even less. Ian asked, "Do you know who these men are?"

"Yes. You aren't going to fucking believe this, one of them is the son of a prominent US Senator and is currently being heavily vetted for a prestigious appointment within the State Department." Mitch looked at both men and just waited. Grant Westmore was the only son of John and Nanette Westmore. They were definitely one of Washington's power couples. John Westmore was well known for his ability to "tie up loose ends" and word on the street was that anyone who managed to get in his way was likely to mysteriously disappear.

It was Jace who responded first. "Fucking Grant Westmore? That little weasel has been put on a pedestal so high he probably gets nosebleeds. How much danger is Callie in?" Ian and Mitch both shook their heads. Leave it to Jace to sum everything up in three sentences and capture the entire essence of the situation.

Mitch wasn't about to hedge. He laid it all out. "Well, you know the kind of clout Nan Westmore's family yields. Hell, her father was one of the most corrupt senators this country has ever elected, and his connections to organized crime are legendary. But it's Senator

Westmore who concerns me the most. He has been known to refer to his son's rape of a young woman five years younger than he was as his 'son's wild night with the local slut.' And it seems he's been on a campaign to smear Callie for some time. He's leaving nothing to chance, he has made sure no one in the hotel industry will hire her despite the fact she was top in her class and the reports from her internship practically glow in the fucking dark. The old bastard has essentially blackballed her career, making her a victim yet again. Oh, and Grant's partner in crime died in a very strange automobile accident less than a year ago. No witnesses, brake failure, convenient timing, you get the idea."

Waiting a few seconds for the information to sink in, Mitch watched as Ian McGregor clenched and unclenched his fists in a show of frustration that Mitch had rarely seen, despite having worked with the man on several very demanding projects. Mitch continued, "The amazing thing is—despite the fact she seems to know what's happening to her career-wise, she has a remarkable work ethic and record. She is genuinely well liked by all of her coworkers, even though most of them wish she'd stand up for herself with her boss. Seems the ass hat takes great pleasure in bullying her. Personally I think he's on the good senator's payroll. Too bad whoever owns that rag doesn't can his happy ass." He looked up at Ian and grinned. *Oh yeah, my friend, I'm betting the dick-twit, as Rissa would say, will be out within the hour.*

"Honestly, I'm worried she's going to be the victim of a *random* mugging gone bad in that nasty-assed neighborhood where she lives. Christ, guys, have you seen the squalor she's been living in? And that sister of hers is a real piece of work, too. She isn't and never has been a student at any university in the United States, and if my math is correct, she's taken in excess of thirty thousand dollars from her sister in the past several years in *assistance* for her fictional college education, prom dresses, etc. Just FYI, Alex and Zach said they are setting up a lottery drawing to see which of us gets to go kick her ass."

Ian and Jace hadn't said much up to this point, but Ian finally said, "Tell them Jace already won that opportunity. He'll be heading out in a couple of weeks. If I wasn't worried about how heartbroken Callie would be if anything happened to her sister, we'd just let Senator Westmore's goons have at her because I'm sure that she's on his list as well." Mitch knew exactly what Ian had planned, the man was thinking so loud he might as well have been shouting his intent out loud. Mitch agreed with Ian, if anyone could scare Chrissy Reece straight and bring the wild child to heel, it was Jace Garrett.

Mitch finally asked when he was going to get to meet Callie. He'd wondered where they'd stashed her during their conversation. Ian smiled and then answered, "She is just now coming down the stairs. I asked a masseuse from Club Isola to come over and see to it she was nicely relaxed for your chat."

Watching Ian lead Callie Reece closer and seat her in front of the monitor, Mitch was immediately struck by how much she reminded him of Bree Hart in spirit, and she was even more petite than his sweet wife, Rissa. *Christ, she looks like a tiny angel. And there is something familiar about her, but what is it?*

Ian spoke first, "Callie, I'd like you to meet Mitch Grayson, he is a friend and colleague. He has quite a lot of experience working with women who have been the victims of different types of violence."

Mitch watched as Ian looked at Callie with an affection that he well recognized. "It's nice to meet you, Callie. I've heard a lot about you." He smiled when he heard her mentally saying she'd just bet he had—*like how she'd tried to sneak on to the island to spy on Ian's kinky party pals, then gotten her ass paddled, then had a meltdown and crushed a glass so that she was now sporting stitches in her palm. Oh yeah, big prize that Calamity Callie was—just ask anyone….her mom…her sister. Pickle fudge, all those As in college and what do I have to show for it? A job I hate, an apartment most homeless people would pass up, a United States senator who thinks I'm the bad guy because his son and a pal raped me, a mom who blames me for screwing up her social life, and a sister who can't seem to get her head out of her ass no matter how much I try to help her.*

When Mitch heard her mentally sigh, he felt a wave of exhaustion wash over him, and he knew it had come directly from the heart of the woman who was over seventeen hundred miles east of him. He had no idea how she could look so together on the outside when she was so utterly broken on the inside. And he also knew she would thrive under the right Master. What he didn't know was if Ian could be that man—the man had some major fissures in his own foundation.

Callie seemed to refocus, and Mitch smiled at her and said, "Callie, if you'll notice, Ian and Jace have left the room." She seemed startled by the realization that she hadn't even registered their departure. "They wanted you to be able to speak with me freely. I assure you, anything you tell me that you do not want me to share with them, will remain confidential—well, unless it relates to your safety, and then I'm afraid I won't feel the obligation to keep that information to myself." He grinned when she smiled. He was grateful his attempt to lighten the mood seemed to have worked.

"I've found that sometimes victims want the significant people in their lives to have the information, but it's just too painful for them to speak the words to someone they know is going to be upset by them. Maybe you understand what I mean? It might be good for Ian and Jace to know what happened, but simply by virtue of the fact that they care about you, you know it would be too difficult to tell them yourself. Does that sound about right?" Mitch knew he'd nailed it when her eyes went as wide as saucers and she merely nodded. Of course he was picking up random pieces now, but her mind had gone pretty blank when she'd realized they were alone. He'd heard women tell him the exact words he'd just spoken to Callie, and for the hundredth time, he was grateful for all those hours he spent working at the women's shelters.

"Could you maybe tell me something about yourself so that I feel like I know you a bit before I tell you anything? Because this is a bit weird, you know?" Mitch knew she was struggling to get her feet under her, because this whole situation had blindsided her.

"Sure, I'm a retired Navy SEAL whose specialty was communications. I am one of two husbands in a polyamorous marriage, and we live in Colorado. My wife Rissa is expecting soon, and she is a fireball. Both Bryant Davis and I are Doms, and Rissa is our submissive as well as our wife. Well, at least she lets us believe she's submissive. Quite frankly, sometimes it's a bit difficult to determine who's running the show—especially right now." He laughed and was relieved to hear her soft laughter. He heard her thoughts clearly now, and he was glad to know she was relaxing and had decided he was genuinely a nice guy who seemed to have her best interests at heart even if he was a pal of Ian's. "How about this? I know it's hard to start, so why don't you tell me about the incident yesterday that prompted Ian to call me?" He saw her glance down at her hand, and when she returned her eyes to his, he could see the unshed tears.

"Well…I got lost in the memory of something that happened to me in high school. And if I was a betting person, I'd bet you already know all about this or we wouldn't be having this conversation." She took a deep breath, and Mitch could see her gathering her resolve. "At the end of my junior year, I went to a beer party down at the river outside of the town where I'd grown up. I didn't drink, and that made some people think I was being a snob. That wasn't it, I just didn't like the taste of beer and I had driven so I knew I couldn't drink. Anyway, when I was walking back to my car, I was ambushed by a couple of drunk guys who were home from college for summer break. They were several years older than I was, but I knew who they were because their families were big shots in our small town." She took several deep breaths, and he could see she was thinking about her next words. He waited patiently while she fiddled with the hem of the shirt she wore. "They raped me, Mr. Grayson. And one of the things I have regretted the most in my life is letting my mother talk me out of pressing charges against them."

Mitch had never wanted to hurt a woman like he wanted to hurt Callie Reece's mother. How any woman could treat her daughter so callously was lost on him. But to do so because of possible damage to your perceived social standing was even more incomprehensible. He waited a few seconds so she wouldn't feel his words were trite and spur of the moment, it was important that she understood he *had* really been listening and his words were the result of the information she'd just given, not hours of previous research. "Callie, first of all, please call me Mitch. I'm curious, why do you think your mom would do that?"

She laughed, but it certainly wasn't a sound of joy. "My mom knew if I reported it, her social standing would be forever damaged. And trust me, Mitch, that was and always will be much more important to my mother than justice for me. She isn't a very nice person, let's just leave it at that. Anyway, I moved in with relatives for my senior year, and they were wonderful to me. For the first time, someone cared more about me than they cared about whether or not they were going to be invited to the Snow Ball at the Country Club." Mitch was relieved when the waves of anxiety that had been coming from Callie during the first part of their talk changed to warmth and love as she spoke about her time with her aunt and uncle.

"Tell me about the family that you moved in with." He wanted to give her a chance to regroup a bit and spending time recalling that time was obviously filled with happy memories and a great way for her to relax.

As she related stories about her time with a family that obviously treated her well, he listened as much to what she didn't say as to what she did. Not once did she mention a visit from her mother or sister. She did mention that she'd talked to her father on the phone weekly, but she'd been fairly sure that had been her aunt's doing.

When he'd asked Callie if she had been contacted by either of the perpetrators or a representative for either of them, her anxiety level went straight through the roof. She said that she hadn't, and Mitch knew she was telling the truth, but he also knew she feared that it was inevitable. He also noticed that she hadn't mentioned the accident that had claimed Charlie Ives's life or the obvious implications that held for her. As an intelligent woman, she would make the connection quickly. But that was news for Ian to share. Mitch's job was to listen.

Chapter 10

It had been several days since Callie had spoken with Mitch Grayson, and she had seemed to relax more after their conversation. He was glad they had been able to remove the sutures from her hand because he had outdoor plans for his little sub. Ian was grateful for the time Mitch had spent with Callie. She had disclosed more than either of them had expected and then had agreed to let Mitch share all of the information with both Ian and Jace. And while Ian would have liked to have heard it directly from her, Mitch had made it abundantly clear that it was more common than not for disclosure to a disinterested third party to be much easier. Mitch had said, "Loved ones react—even when they don't intend to—and victims are very sensitive to those reactions." It actually made perfect sense once Mitch had explained it, but there was still a small piece of him that was a Dom to the core and that Dom demanded her unconditional surrender.

Jace had reminded him that surrender involves trust and trust has to be earned. Damned if he didn't hate it when someone else was right. He didn't remember how many times he'd told the Doms he was training at Club Isola that very same thing—probably hundreds—but that didn't make it any easier to hear.

Ian had been particularly relieved when Mitch assured him that Callie was not lying about anything that he could determine. Mitch had promised to forward all his information immediately, and he'd smiled at Ian before asking, "Weren't you looking for a manager for a resort you were planning to build if the right person came along?"

"Smart-ass. Yes, you know I have been looking, and yes, I am interested in talking to her about the position if things work out to that end." When he looked at Mitch's smiling face, he just shook his head. *Christ, is everybody a fucking matchmaker all the sudden. My friends start getting married, and all of the sudden they paint a target on me as well.*

Ian had sent Callie up to the bedroom with instructions to take a short nap and then dress in the swimsuit he'd laid out for her. He and Jace had both laughed when she'd looked baffled and then said, "But I didn't pack a swimsuit. I don't even own one anymore because in my neighborhood that wouldn't even be something I'd want anyone to know I had, let alone I'd actually wear anywhere."

* * * *

Walking toward the beach, Ian kept a hand on Callie at all times. It was a standard training technique, but it was also something he enjoyed doing with the submissives he'd trained because he found it kept them grounded to him and made his commands easier for them to follow. But today there was something different. He didn't feel like he had with other subs. It wasn't the same when he had known that he was training them with the intent to hand them over to another Dom. The thought of any Dom other than Jace commanding Callie made each and every muscle in his body become tense and something akin to jealousy surge through his blood.

As he led her down the stone steps to the sandy beach, he'd been talking to her about the importance of honesty and full disclosure in D/s relationships. "I want you to understand that the dynamics of a Dominant and submissive's relationship is significantly more intense than that of two people who are just dating for several reasons. The level of trust required is exponentially higher because there are levels of play that can result in severe injury if certain safety measures aren't followed strictly. Knowing exactly what a scene is going to entail through negotiation is an important element, particularly in the beginning." He chuckled and drew her into his arms for a swift hug before adding, "Now, your situation is unique, my lovely pet, because you aren't at liberty to pick and choose which Dom you get to play with like an uncollared sub at a club ordinarily would. Oh no, my little *Carlin*, you belong only to me."

Ian couldn't resist her for another minute, he leaned down and pressed his lips against hers and kissed her. What started as a sweet kiss quickly turned into pure lustful desire. When he pulled back, he looked thoughtfully into her eyes and said, "I would like nothing more than to sink into your silken heat right now, but I have a plan and I'm going to follow it." And then more to himself than to her, he added, "Even if it fucking kills me."

Callie giggled as they continued walking toward the water's edge, and Ian simply smiled. "You laugh now, pet, but you'll see soon enough that I'm not very patient when comes to fucking you when the notion strikes me. And you'll always be at my command, and you'll always make sure I have unfettered access to what is now mine." When they reached a large blanket laid out on the sand, he motioned for her to join him.

"I mentioned the importance of complete honesty, and I want you to know that works both ways—at least as it relates to life events, etc. I will reserve the right to withhold information I feel may cause you harm or something I'm keeping secret for a surprise, but I won't ever lie to you, and I'll tell you things I know that are of importance to you, even if I'd rather spare you the emotional upset I'm sure they are going to cause." He could see her eyes go wide with concern, and he hated the fact that he was going to have to tell her things he knew were going to be devastating to the tiny angel in front of him.

As he proceeded to explain what her sister had recently revealed to friends about the money their mother had demanded from the Westmore and Ives families, he saw her emotions swing from disbelief to horror and then to rage. "I can't begin to tell you how sorry I am to tell you these things about your family, but I can't very

well demand your honesty if I'm not willing to give you the same."
Stroking his fingers lightly over her cheek, he wiped away her tears.

"How could she do something so horrible? She all but told them I
was pregnant and going to need the money to raise the child. Oh my
God, what if people thought I was going to get an abortion? How
could she be so callous? I mean, I knew she blamed me for everything
that happened, but this? This is so much worse. And Chrissy knew
this and didn't tell me?"

Sighing deeply, Ian pulled Callie on to his lap. "About your
sister—it appears that she is not, nor has she ever been a college
student. She is in fact working as an exotic dancer in Miami and
making an obscene amount of money, I might add. After some
investigation we know exactly how much money you have given her
over the years, and I promise you, pet, she is going to be made
accountable for each and every cent." His heart was nearly torn in two
as her tiny body was racked by great gulping sobs. There wasn't
anything he could say, he just held her and let her purge the emotion
from her soul.

When she finally began to quiet down, he pulled her back so that
he was looking into her face again, and as if sensing he had more to
say, she started crying again. "Please, oh please don't tell me there is
more. I can't take any more, I swear to you, I just can't."

"The rest is not so bad, pet, I promise you. And I want all of this
garbage out on the table so we can start with each other with a clean
slate." When he saw acceptance in her eyes, he continued. "Now, the
tabloid you work for is wholly owned by McGregor Holdings, Inc."
He smiled when her eyes went wide. "Oh yes, I can see it in your
eyes, you understand exactly what that means don't you, pet?"
Laughing at her slow nod, he went on, "Well, not only does it mean
you are, for the indeterminate future, assigned to this project, it also
means that your boss is no longer employed by the paper I had been
considering dismantling anyway. His days of bullying you are over,
and he was none too happy with how it all went down, I can assure

you. Quite frankly, Mitch, Jace, and I all feel it's likely he was already working for Senator Westmore and that his efforts to get you hurt were actually orchestrated attempts to tie up loose ends to ease his son's political progress."

Ian would have given anything at that moment to have been able to wipe away the utter defeat he saw in her expression. "I hope you don't dismantle the paper entirely. There are a lot of good people working there, and without Bob assigning ridiculous stories, I think they can do some good things for the community. Some of those people have been working there a long time, and it would difficult for them to find other jobs in this economy."

Wrapping his arms around her, he gave her a tight squeeze. "Do your friends realize how lucky they are to have you? You never cease to amaze me. Your concern for others warms my heart. Considering all of the various types of people that I deal with, you are a very welcome change. But, we need to get back to our training or things aren't going to go well for you tonight. Up you go."

After Ian had gotten up, he reached into the small box sitting at the edge of the blanket and pulled out a bottle of water. "Drink this, you're going to need to stay hydrated, I have a lot planned for you in the hours to come." Once she'd downed most of the bottle, he set it aside and turned to her and simply said, "Strip."

* * * *

When they had left the house earlier, Callie had searched his eyes for any sort of clue as to what Ian was thinking. As they approached a beautiful expanse of glistening white sand, Callie worried about the tension that seemed to be radiating off him. No doubt, Mitch Grayson had already shared everything she'd told him. Likely he was just leading her out here in order to let her know he was no longer interested. After all, her mom had told her time and again that if any man found out what had happened he would consider her tainted goods and wouldn't want her. So her only questions now were, how do I keep him at a safe distance? *If I take myself out it hurts less than being rejected.* And now how do I get the story?

As Ian had continued what he kept referring to as a lesson in trust, she'd become more and more depressed. How could her family have betrayed her on so many levels? Truthfully, the information about her mother wasn't all that surprising since Callie had always known her mother had only cared about herself, but her sister's betrayal was devastating. She didn't have any idea how to even begin to deal with that situation. *Do I confront her? Do I demand she return the money? Damn, I lived in that hellhole so I could help her. Why would she do this to me?* She suddenly realized she'd been speaking out loud, and when she looked up into Ian's eyes, they were blazing with frustration.

"We have a problem, *Carlin*. You aren't 'present,' and I need you to be here with me or we can't do this, do you understand?" She could only manage to nod her head, and then he continued speaking. "Nods and shakes of the head are not good enough, pet. You must always speak your answers so that we maintain clear lines of communication and there is no doubt that you understood the question. So, try again, and the proper answer is always 'Yes, Sir' or 'Yes, Master Ian.'"

Callie wasn't surprised by the instruction, she had done enough research that she knew some of the rules and protocol. She hadn't needed to learn it for the story, but she'd gotten so caught up in it as she was reading that she hadn't been able to stop at the bare minimum that might have been needed. Looking directly at him, she spoke softly, but clearly. "Yes, Master, I understand." She could tell her answer pleased him by the smile that went over his face, and suddenly pleasing him became her sole objective for the rest of this scene.

When he stepped back from her and told her once again to strip, she didn't even think about the fact that they were outside. She quickly removed the string bikini she'd been wearing, and when she handed it to Ian, she noticed he was holding a blindfold. "I'm going to cover your eyes because I want you to concentrate on my voice and the words I'm speaking to you. I don't want you distracted by what you see. You need to focus on what you are feeling." He paused for long seconds before continuing. "And for the record, your sister is going to make this up to you. I promise you that. Jace will be traveling to Miami later to deal with her. Mitch Grayson, along with a few more of our friends in Colorado, weren't at all happy that they were left out of what they had set up as a lottery to see who got to go. Seems you make loyal friends pretty quickly, my beautiful pet." He'd been running his fingers through her hair, beginning with soft massaging strokes to her scalp, and she'd quickly found herself almost hypnotized by his voice.

After securing the blindfold, he'd run his fingers through folds of her pussy, and she knew exactly what he'd found. She'd felt herself creaming from the time they'd stood up and she'd known the scene was officially starting.

"Oh, pet, you are so wonderfully wet for me. That pleases me more than I can tell you. Now, I'm going to show you two more poses. The first is what I will refer to as the slave pose." He'd helped her to her knees and shown her how he wanted her forehead to touch the ground with her arms stretched out in front of her and her ass displayed high in the air. She didn't even want to think about how that had to look from the house. *Geez, Callie, nothing like flashing your who-ha for all to see.*

"*Carlin*, the only person you need to worry about is me. Remember, your job is to place yourself into my care…it's all about trust, don't forget that." He chuckled just a bit and then added, "And yes, you did indeed say that out loud." He had kept a hand on her at all times, and that was all that kept her from being frightened, but his touch and his words kept her tethered to the reality of placing herself into his care, and it was oddly liberating.

As if he'd read her thoughts, he'd leaned down and whispered, "It's freeing isn't it, pet? You don't have to worry about anything except doing as I command you. You don't have to be concerned with any of the details that usually plague women. No need to wonder if you're doing too much or too little—if you should initiate a kiss or take my hand." She felt a shiver snake up her spine as his fingers moved from her ass to the nape of her neck.

"Not all Doms use the same names for this pose, but it is one of the poses I'll use with you quite a bit so I want you to memorize exactly how it feels." He left her like that for several minutes, but never stopped touching her. When she felt her muscles start to relax into the position, he leaned close to her ear and she felt his warm breath brush over her skin like a soft breeze. His voice was pure seduction when he said, "Good girl. Now, up you go." After she'd gotten back up on her feet, he smiled at her when she weaved slightly as blood rushed from her head. "Easy, pet. This is one of the reasons a good Dom keeps his hands on his sub at all times. There are a lot of times when you may be unsteady for a variety of reasons, but it is also important for you to know I am always close. One of the cardinal rules of D/s play is that a sub is *never* left alone during a scene, particularly if the sub is bound in any way. I am a fan of the Japanese art of rope bondage known as Kinbaku. I enjoy both Shinju, or breast bondage, and Karada, which encompasses the entire body, and suspension that offers erotic stimulation with the slightest movement is something I look forward to introducing you to when the time is right. But we'll be working on trust for a long while before I will take you to the erotic plane that the people of the Orient were enjoying for centuries before the rest of us had a clue."

Callie could hear his respect for the art clearly in his voice, and she'd seen a few pictures of rope play but hadn't understood the attraction until she heard the reverence in Ian's voice. She found herself leaning in to his touch, and when he gripped her arms, she realized she had been close to collapsing on to him. His words warmed her and assured her that she wasn't in trouble for her lapse in attention. "You are so fucking beautiful and more responsive than I could ever have hoped." He continued stroking up and down her arms for several seconds. His touch allowed her to focus on how his hands felt against her skin as the sun warmed her. She could smell the water of the bay and hear the waves as they slowly lapped at the beach's edge. The mournful sound of a boat's horn in the distance and the breeze as it cooled her warm skin all added to the ambiance of the moment. She could hear the soft sounds of a waterfall somewhere in the distance, and it soothed her. "Good girl. You finally let yourself just float in the moment, and it felt wonderful to know that I was caring for you in all ways, didn't it?"

"Yes, Master. It did." She felt Ian go still at her answer, and she was afraid she'd said something wrong. "I'm sorry, did I do something wrong?" She started to reach for the blindfold, she needed to be able to see his face, but he grabbed her wrists and stopped her.

"No, quite the opposite actually, but you surprised me, and that doesn't happen very often, I assure you. Your words were a huge gift that you will understand later. But right now I want to teach you the punishment pose. You aren't being punished, I just want you to understand how to assume this position should you be instructed to do so. And I will caution you, if Jace or I instruct you to do this, it had better be immediate, because your punishment will be increased significantly for any hesitation or delay."

After he'd shown her how far apart he wanted her legs and how to bend at the waist, she knew that both her ass and her pussy were wide open for anything he'd want to do, and she was shocked at how much the idea turned her on. While she was in this position, she heard the snick of what sounded like a bottle and quickly felt cool, slick lube being dribbled over her back entrance. His finger started rimming her ass, and then he slowly started pushing past the ring of resistance. She heard herself moan and knew she was getting lost in the feel of the heat as her muscles stretched to accommodate his invasion. She'd been so caught up in feeling how the pain changed into pleasure she hadn't even realized he'd withdrawn his fingers until she felt the plug as he started slow thrusts and retreats.

"Tell me how it feels, pet. I want to hear your words." She was almost as caught up in his voice as she was the feelings racing through her body like a runaway train.

"It feels...so hot and naughty and amazing. I know that you are touching me in a place that no one else gets to see. The burning changes to need, and I don't understand it, but I know you do, so I am just enjoying the power of the feeling."

"Fucking perfect. Pet, you are going to wear this plug until either Master Jace or I remove it. Now, I want you to stand up slowly." As she brought her head up, she felt herself sway and was grateful for his support. When she shifted slightly, the plug in her ass moved and she felt her knees go out from under her. He chuckled as he grabbed her around the waist. "Tell me how it feels with that plug inside your ass, pet. Does it make you feel wanton?"

"Oh God, I feel...oh, I just feel like I want to..." She couldn't focus or get the words to come out in any sort of reasonable order.

Suddenly she felt a sharp swat to her ass, and everything shifted again. "Answer the question, pet, or I'll bend you right back over and administer a few swats that will more than center your attention."

It took her a couple of seconds, but she finally answered in a hesitant and halting voice that, even to her own ears, sounded nearly breathless. "It makes me feel an incredible need to be fucked, Sir."

"Aww, see that wasn't so hard, now was it? And just so you know, pet, you answer was perfect. We are right where I wanted us to be. Now, there are some rules I want you to know about before we go to the club tonight. Pay attention, these will keep you from getting into trouble once we enter the first of the two areas I'm going to show you tonight. There are three zones at Club Isola, but you'll only be visiting two for your first several visits. I want to make sure you are properly prepared before taking you in to the Inferno Room. That is where the most extreme play takes place. I don't play there often, but it is a popular area and I'll want you to understand what happens there." *I'm not sure that is a place I'll ever be ready to see. It sounds much too extreme for my comfort.*

He was running his fingers through her folds and circling around her clit but never giving her the touch she was craving, and she was starting to move just enough to get his fingers to slide over the little bundle of nerves that she knew would put her over the edge. "Please..." She heard her voice, but didn't remember speaking.

"Not yet, pet. Don't you dare come until I give you permission, if you do, I'll punish you, right out here for the men on the boat passing by to see. They are standing on the deck admiring you. They want what is mine, but I'll not share your lovely cunt with anyone but Jace. And when he and I fuck you together, we're going to give you so much pleasure, you'll think you are being given a glimpse of heaven." He had leaned forward so that his words were spoken directly into her ear and just as he ended he bit down on her earlobe and said, "Come for me, pet."

The only thing Callie remembered was hearing a scream and then feeling as if her entire body had exploded. She fell against Ian and felt her cream rush toward his waiting fingers. It took her several deep breaths to bring herself back from what had been an amazing voyage into a colorful supernova. When she finally started to settle, she realized she was sitting in his lap and he was speaking to her tenderly, telling her how proud he was of her and those words alone brought tears to her eyes.

When he slowly rose to his feet, she realized that he was carrying her into the water. "As I explain more of the rules, I'm going to be securing you to a new device I'm developing. If it works as I expect it to, you're going to really enjoy it." As he set her on what felt like a large pillow, he began talking to her about how she would not be allowed to wear panties or shoes at any time while inside Club Isola. He explained how she would be expected to keep her gaze lowered unless a she was specifically instructed to raise it. He also told her that he would be securing a temporary collar around her neck in order to protect her from the unwanted advances she would most certainly be getting without that mark of his ownership and protection.

She was listening and hearing the words, but she didn't know how much of the meaning she really comprehended when she was so lost in all the sensations. He'd secured her arms above her head and her feet to some kind of extensions that kept her legs spread wide apart. The feeling of the sun's warmth and the water's sensuous caress on her bared pussy was strangely erotic.

"I am introducing you to the BDSM lifestyle with every move, every word, every caress, and every press of my body against yours. Remember that even the deepest ocean begins at the beach. How deep you venture depends on your own level of comfort." She'd heard his words, and their meaning had seemed particularly poignant even though she didn't understand exactly why.

Chapter 11

As Ian secured Callie to the floating cross, he found himself staring at the woman lying open to his every pleasure and wondering if it was possible that he'd been wrong all these years when he'd been so certain he was incapable of truly loving anyone again. Nolyn McGregor, now Nolyn Bieberle, had been the embodiment of every horrible cliché ever written about stepmothers, with a dash of pedophile added in for good measure. She'd invaded his bed when he'd been too young to understand the significance of the darkness she was exposing him to. Nolyn's need for pain had fueled his fantasies and introduced him to elements of the lifestyle that had become the center of his sexual identity from the first time she'd shown him how Domination could open up what was locked deep inside of him.

Years of what he now recognized as sexual abuse at her hand had not only thrust him into *The Land of Kink* at a ridiculously young age but had also built a high wall between Ian and his father that had taken years to breach. That wall had only started to truly crumble just before his father had died too young and Ian had been forced to assume the role of CEO for a company that was on the very cusp of financial collapse.

Ian had been grateful that Nolyn had been well and truly out of the picture when his father passed so he hadn't had to deal with her as far as the estate had been concerned, but it had been surprisingly difficult to see her at the memorial service. Despite everything that had occurred, he had loved her in his own twisted and naive way. He'd been devastated to learn she hadn't ever planned to leave his father for him and that he wasn't the only rich "boy toy" she'd play with. He had vowed he would never trust another woman with his heart, and he'd held tightly to that promise ever since. But in the deepest part of his consciousness, something told him that Callie Reece might well be his kryptonite.

Moving his hands over her body in what she would perceive as random patterns, Ian was actually slowly focusing all of her energy on her sex. By the time she understood what the sensuous massage had been about, she was so caught up in the sensations he was creating she was helpless to put up any barriers. "Tell me, pet, what does it feel like to know that you are completely open to my perusal just as you are to the warming rays of the sun and the lapping waters of the bay?"

Callie groaned and then spoke the words he'd been hoping to hear. "It feels delicious. I know it shouldn't, that good girls don't show everyone their privates, but it just feels so hot when I know you are controlling who sees me."

He was sure he'd never had a submissive give him a more perfect answer, and what little blood had been left in his brain raced south to join the rest. He quickly maneuvered the floating frame into shallow water and pushed his cock deep in one thrust. He felt her rippling heat surround and squeeze him, and he worried the entire scene was going to end in a thirty-second pounding if he didn't rein himself in quickly.

Deliberately distracting himself with accounting figures was helping, but her softly whispered pleas of need were quickly swamping his control. Pulling from her body in a slow withdrawal intended to let her feel every vein and ridge of his cock, he watched as her body involuntarily arched upward. God, she was the most beautiful woman he'd ever seen. Even without being able to see her eyes, he knew they were dilated with need and would be seeking his as she rose closer and closer to release.

Just as he knew she was reaching a point where she wouldn't be able to call back the climax, he set a fast pace, fucking her with a desperation that was totally unfamiliar to him. "Come for me, Callie. Come now." Her muscles tightened around him with an almost viselike grip, and her scream was immediate. He managed several more thrusts before he followed her over the edge of a canyon of release so deep he wasn't sure he was going to be able to remain standing. Locking his knees and gripping the floating cross was the only thing that kept him from drowning in the pleasure and the sun-warmed, salty water of the bay. Whether or not she knew it, the beautiful pixie lying before him had just stolen his heart and soul.

* * * *

Walking up to the well-shrouded entrance of Club Isola, Callie was completely enchanted by the beautifully carved figures surrounding ornately decorated doors that were easily ten feet tall. She felt as if she were being led into some ancient mystical tomb. Grecian planters filled with trailing vines and small white flowers softened the look just enough to keep it from being overly intimidating. The dress Ian had given her to wear tonight reminded her of the sheers her mother used to hang over their windows when she'd been a child, except that the dress was a soft shade of violet that complemented her eyes and accented the light kiss of the sun her skin had gotten this afternoon on the beach. She loved the jeweled sandals he'd given her and was hesitant to relinquish them once they'd entered the reception area of the club.

A vibrant woman with skin the color of dark caramel and dancing dark eyes greeted them, and Callie felt herself immediately drawn to her. Ian had introduced her to Dee and explained that she and her husband, Mike, were among the few people that lived on the island full-time. Dee had assured her that she would personally watch over her new shoes, so she had slowly handed them over. She knew it was ridiculous to have become so attached to them, but it had been so long since she'd had anything new and pretty that it had seemed like she was having them snatched from her when she'd been told to hand them over.

Ian pulled her to the side and brushed her hair back over her shoulder and stared in to her eyes before asking, "Tell me what that was about, pet. I've never seen a sub so sad to hand over a pair of shoes. Help me understand what was going through your mind." She could see that he was truly troubled by her reaction, and she hated knowing she was risking ruining their evening because she liked a pair of shoes.

She took a deep breath and decided that total honesty was her only option. "It's just that…well, it's been such a long time since I had anything new and they are so pretty and I really like them….and well, the last time I had a new pair of shoes, Chrissy decided she wanted them and I didn't have enough backbone to say no." She hated feeling like a whining child, but she knew he would have seen through anything other than the truth.

Ian's expression softened, and his eyes didn't reflect the pity she had dreaded seeing. Instead, all she saw was compassion. "Your honesty pleases me very much, pet. And while it saddens me that you have waited so long for pretty things, it humbles me to know I've provided you with something you like enough that you are concerned about losing it. The fact is, most of the women I meet, both here and in my various business associations, are spoiled beyond belief. So knowing that you find satisfaction in a small gift speaks very highly about who you are. Thank you for letting me see that very important piece of you." His words sent warmth clear to her soul, and she found herself leaning her cheek into his palm, losing herself in the pleasure of knowing she'd pleased him.

Entering the main lounge area of the club, Callie was amazed at how enormous the room was. It was in fact a large natural stone cavern, and the glow of the wall lighting highlighted the layers of vibrant color lacing the stone walls. The bar at the left reminded her of the ones she'd seen in old movies, all dark wood and sparkling glasses hanging from overhead racks. The dark-skinned man behind the bar was huge. He had to stand at least six and a half feet tall, and his chest was massive. The leather vest he wore drew attention to arms that rippled with muscles, and she wondered for just a moment if his enormous hands could wrap themselves completely around a basketball. As she and Ian approached, the man looked up, and she felt herself freeze in place. She'd have had to live on another planet to not recognize the face looking at her as if she were something to snack on. Mike Tate had been a star in the NFL for years, and his decision to retire had stunned the sports world.

Ian had gently tugged her hand and leaned toward her and said, "He's big, but he's really a teddy bear, although Dee might swear otherwise on occasion. Come along, I want to introduce you." When they'd gotten close to the bar, Ian had lifted her and set her very bare ass on the barstool and smiled at her quick gasp when the cool leather met her warm skin. He leaned forward and kissed the end of her nose then smiled. "I love hearing that startled gasp as you become aware your warm little pussy is bared for your Master." Then he turned to the man who stood watching their interaction. "Mike, I'd like you to meet Callie Reece, Callie this is Mike Tate, humbly known as Dee's loving husband and Dom."

Mike Tate reached forward when she extended her hand, and she watched as his swamped hers. "It is a pleasure to meet you, Mr. Tate. And while I am sure claiming Dee as your own is a worthy accomplishment, I assure you, I'm well aware that it is not your only claim to fame. And I will take great pleasure in letting my fellow Monday night football friends know I've gotten to meet you in person."

Ian was staring at her with something between shock and awe, and Mike Tate leaned his head back and roared in laughter. "Well, Nixie, I don't believe I have ever seen the boss speechless before." The man patted Ian on the shoulder with the bear paw at the end of his arm and said, "It's okay, boss-man, it's always the ones you least expect."

Callie knew she wasn't supposed to speak without permission, but she couldn't stop the words. "You called me a water sprite, why?" And now the big man was a speechless as Ian had been a moment earlier.

"Holy shit, Ian—she's a natural sub, beautiful, a football fan, and knows her mythical literature. Christ, man, you'd better marry her quick—she's fucking perfect. And I called you a water sprite because I was on perimeter this afternoon, which means I check all the beaches on the island." He waited for a few beats until he saw realization in her eyes and then he laughed again. "You are beautiful, sweetness, so you should not be embarrassed that your Master was sharing a glimpse of that beauty with those of us who happened to be lucky enough to wander close." Then turning to Ian, he added, "And, boss-man, it looks like your latest invention is a resounding success. Better get the patents going on that ASAP." With that, he turned to his other customers and left Callie staring after him.

Ian swiveled her stool so she was turned to face him, and she was relieved that he was smiling. "Well, my pet, it seems you have made quite an impression on yet another of my friends. I must say, it is easy to see why your coworkers speak so highly of you. I've also read your internship reports, and I'd like to talk with you about those in the next few days. But for now, let's take a walk around and see what you think of Club Isola."

Chapter 12

Walking through the main areas of Club Isola reminded Callie just how *in over her head* she really was. Ian drew people like a magnet, and it was easy to see how respected he was among the club's members. And Callie was particularly aware of how amazing he was. When she'd walked down the stairs this evening and seen him waiting for her at the bottom, she'd felt a myriad of desire, longing, and lust. His black slacks, shirt, and shoes were both sophisticated and powerful without being overstated. He appeared both professional and dominant, not to mention truly drool-worthy.

As they walked through the room, Ian greeted everyone and introduced her to many of the most prominent figures in and around Washington's political scene. Suddenly it made perfect sense that her boss would be working for Senator Westmore. She didn't doubt for a minute that the senator would like nothing more than to know exactly who the patrons of Club Isola were. He'd be able to leverage the information against them, it was common knowledge that information was power and in the wrong hands it was lethal.

She watched as people seemed to gravitate toward Ian and how he easily brought out the best in the people he interacted with. It utterly charmed her to see how well liked he was. The uncollared subs were all vying for his attention, and she sensed his attention had just painted a very large target on her back. For just a second, she wondered if any of them would report her whereabouts to Senator Westmore. And would the good senator be able to buy Ian off as he had everyone else she'd ever gotten close to? Callie had no idea what she had done that brought Ian's full attention to her, but he stopped suddenly and faced her. Tipping her chin up so that he could look directly into her eyes, he asked, "What was that thought, *Carlin*?"

"Oh…nothing of any significance, really. You have an amazing club, you know? How you managed to incorporate elegance, and the natural feeling of a cave is pure genius." She started to squirm when he didn't respond, but continued to just watch her. She knew she hadn't answered honestly, but she was so tired of being afraid, and she wanted to just enjoy the evening. She only had a month with Ian, and she didn't want to waste any of that time thinking about what she had to return to in just a few weeks. Her hope that lying low until Grant Westmore's career was secure would be enough to remove the target was probably pure folly, but it was really the only sliver of hope she had left.

* * * *

Ian had always been keenly attuned to any submissive he was training, but his connection to Callie was particularly powerful. He'd felt the anxiety wash through her as if it had been ice moving through her entire body. He knew she was trying to hide it and just enjoy her evening, and while he appreciated the effort on one level, as her Dom he had no intention of letting her conceal something that was obviously so troubling.

He hadn't done a demonstration in the club in months for several reasons. As the owner of Club Isola, the pressure on him and the sub he used was always tremendous. And everything else in the club tended to come to a complete standstill because everyone crowded around to watch. He turned to Jace and simply nodded. Watching as Callie's eyes became worried and watchful, he leaned forward and kissed her on the forehead before saying, "Come," and then grasping her tiny hand, he led her to the small stage.

He left her standing at the bottom of the stairs and moved to speak with Jace before returning for her. He wanted Jace to alert the rest of the security team that he wanted them watching the crowd, not the scene. His internal alarms were blaring that there was someone among tonight's players who would be forwarding information to Senator Westmore. All electronic equipment was banned from inside the club, but it wasn't inconceivable that someone would try to take a picture to send later. The rules of membership clearly stated that you were immediately banned for life if it became known that you had used any type of device while inside the club. But if anyone was caught trying to take a picture of Callie, he'd personally see to it that being banned from the most exclusive BDSM club on the east coast was the least of their worries.

He had planned to do a small demonstration tonight, but Callie had given him the perfect reason to step things up a bit. Returning to his very nervous sub, Ian lightly touched her check before speaking. "I had already planned to do a scene with you tonight, it isn't something I do often, and you'll quickly see why that is. But our focus is now changed a bit. I'm going to put on a mic so that I can also use this as a teaching tool because there are several new Doms here tonight. But remember, I will always protect your privacy and when the time comes, I'll switch it off, because what you have to say belongs only to me."

What Ian hadn't told her was that it was the sadness he'd seen linger in her expression after he'd asked about her thoughts that had caused him to change the focus of his scene. Everyone in her life had betrayed her—well, everyone save one family in Kansas, so it was easy to see why trust was such an issue for her. He could have punished her for not answering honestly, but that wouldn't have done anything to promote the trust he'd been talking to her about all day. Ian clipped the small mic to his shirt but didn't activate it. "Are you ready, pet?"

"Yes, Master. Well, at least I think so." She glanced nervously around her as people quickly began to gather.

"Callie, during this scene I want you to keep your eyes on me at all times. If you don't think you can do that, just tell me and I'll blindfold you. I won't always give you an option, but because this is new to you I want you as comfortable as possible. Would this be easier for you if you were blindfolded?" He waited patiently as her eyes seemed to be searching the crowd that had gathered. He placed his hands along the sides of her face and used his thumbs to brush soothing strokes over her cheeks. "It's okay, pet. You aren't being punished, I'm just going to take this opportunity to help you break down some of your barriers and be completely open with me." The relief that he saw in her eyes had been so complete he was grateful he'd taken the time to speak with her despite the fact their audience was waiting nearby.

"Oh yes, I think a blindfold would be a good idea...and...well, thank you...Master. I know I can get lost in your voice if I'm not worrying about what all those people are saying."

"Very well." Ian reached up and activated the mic and saw her wince as the speakers around the stage clicked on. "As most of you know, I don't often do public scenes and rarely do training demos outside of a formal training setting. But tonight a situation has presented itself with my beautiful submissive, and I'm going to use it as an opportunity to show you how you can coax information from a reluctant submissive." Turning to Callie, his words were softly spoken, but the command was unmistakable. "Strip, pet." He watched as she slid the spaghetti straps of her dress off her dainty shoulders and then slowly lowered the dress so that she could step out of it, every bit the graceful lady she didn't believe herself to be. When Jace stepped forward and held out his hand, she didn't hesitate to hand him the beautiful dress Daph had sent for her.

He just stood and watched her for several seconds as her nipples drew up even tighter under his gaze, but she was obviously completely distracted by the crowd. Ian nodded to Jace again and his friend moved Callie to the box frame and began securing her ankles to the bottom corners and each of her wrists to the top.

Addressing the audience, Ian said, "As you can see, my beautiful pet has been secured to a box frame. What you may not realize is that this frame was made earlier today specifically for her. She is very petite, and our regular frame would have put unnecessary strain on her hips and shoulders. As her Dom, it is my responsibility to make sure the proper equipment is in place for any scene I have planned." He moved to her and double-checked that the cuffs around her wrists were properly secured and then leaned down and double-checked each of the ankle bindings as well.

"Most of you know Jace Garrett and know that he is a skilled Dominant. So my double checking the cuffs is not a reflection of him, it is simply something each Dom should always do regularly throughout a scene. You need to also remind your sub that if at any time they feel tingling or numbness of any kind, they need to alert you immediately." Standing in front of Callie, Ian kissed each of her eyelids and then began securing the blindfold so that she was quickly shrouded in darkness.

"Since my beautiful pet is so new to this lifestyle, you'll notice that I will not ever be more than one step from her and most of the time I will make sure I'm touching her so that she remains grounded in the security of my care. Callie was briefed on the club safe words this afternoon, but I'm going to double-check now to make sure she remembers what she learned." Leaning close to her, he licked up the side of her neck and then kissed the tender spot behind her ear. "Tell me what your safe word is, pet, and when you are supposed to use it."

"I'm using the club's safe word which is *red*, Master. And I am supposed to use it when I can no longer endure whatever is happening. I can also use *yellow* if I need things to slow down or I have a question." Ian was so pleased, her answer had been textbook perfect and the airy quality of her voice had gone straight to his cock.

Using the backs of his fingers, he stroked the side of her face and then trailed his hand slowly down until he could gently pinch her nipples, bringing them back to hard points immediately. "Your answer pleased me very much, pet. You are so very responsive, and your breasts peak to my touch beautifully." He let his fingers slide slowly down until he was moving them back and forth through her slick sex. "Are you wet for me, pet?"

"Yes, Master." He knew she was already starting to zero her focus entirely on his voice, and he wished that they were in his playroom at home so he could just sink into her slick heat. He wouldn't fuck her in public yet, she wasn't ready for that. But he was planning to send her directly in to orgasmic orbit—several times if everything went according to plan.

"You are lovely all spread out for your Master to view. Your body is open and welcomes my touch. Your mind may resist, but your body recognizes its Master and prepares itself for my possession." All the time he'd been speaking he'd continued touching her with soft strokes to the areas he'd noted were particularly sensitive for her.

Ian turned to address the audience again. "You see that Jace has handed me a flogger. Note that this particular instrument has fairly short strips of an extremely soft leather. I'll be using this to sensitize my lovely submissive's skin. I want bring the blood closer to the surface so that she'll feel every touch with a heightened sense of awareness." He used the flogger to tickle her with small flicks of his wrist before actually setting a slow pace of strokes that would be warming without feeling painful. Ian had often heard submissives describe this phase of flogging as "setting the mood" or teasing, so he knew Callie would be falling quickly under the spell of the endorphins that were no doubt flooding her bloodstream.

"How does it feel, pet? Your skin is turning a lovely shade of pink and is warming up nicely." He ran his fingers between her legs, and she coated them with her sweet syrup.

"Oh…it stings, but it turns warm and wonderful. I don't really have words to describe it, Master." Ian listened to the need in her voice and resumed the slow but steady slaps of the leather over her skin.

Pausing in front of her, Ian slid his fingers around each nipple before letting them move down her trembling torso. At her slit, he circled her swollen clit and then slid two fingers into her core and began pressing on the spongy spot. Just as he knew she was about to climax, he pulled his fingers out just far enough that she was moaning at the loss. "My precious pet, I asked you a question earlier this evening and you were less than forthright in your response, do you remember this?"

Ian was standing directly in front of Callie, leaning down so that his lips were brushing against her ear as he spoke. Glancing up, he noticed a woman at the back of the room holding something up to her face. Even though he couldn't see what it was, there was something odd about her body language that set off his internal alarms. His problem was going to be alerting his staff without also alerting the woman or frightening Callie. Ian signaled Jace to approach and clicked off his mic as he circled Callie's ear with his tongue. He had always prided himself on focusing all of his attention on the woman he was playing with so dividing his attention between Callie, Jace, and watching the woman at the back of the room felt wrong and he didn't like it.

As Jace approached, Ian turned his head slightly and nipped the tender spot where Callie's neck met her shoulder and pushed his fingers deep into her channel, hoping to distract her. He turned his face and whispered to Jace. "Back of the room, brunette, two o'clock." Jace was the consummate professional, he smiled and nodded and then headed back to the cabinet where they kept supplies as if he'd been sent to bring another instrument of pleasure to Ian. Ian saw him key his mic and relay the information. It didn't seem that their target had been alerted, but Callie sure as hell had been.

Chapter 13

Callie had been lost in the pleasure and floating toward release when she had felt Ian go rigid against her. The tension literally radiated from him like heat waves off Kansas sidewalks in the summertime. But when he hadn't said anything, she had started to relax again. When he nipped at her shoulder, she'd felt her body release a flood of moisture to coat the fingers he'd pushed inside her. She's been right on the cusp of falling into orgasm when she'd heard Ian whisper to Jace about someone at the back of the room and known instantly that her earlier gut feeling had been right. There was obviously someone in the room working for Senator Westmore. And she'd just handed the most evil man she'd ever known the perfect ammunition to finish her off. His efforts to destroy her had been systematic over the years, but she had always managed to stay true to herself and not give him anything *factual* to use against her. She'd always played by the rules and *behaved* in public…but this? This was going to be just what he had always needed to completely discredit her.

The only thing she could think of was getting out of the restraints holding her naked in front of so many people. The sudden humiliation of her position was making her almost sick to her stomach. "Let me go…please." She knew she sounded like a frightened child, and right at this moment she didn't care.

"Hang on, pet. I promise to get you where you need to go. Just let me—" Ian's words were cut off by Callie's softly whispered words.

"Red, Sir." She knew her body had completely shut out all of the sexual stimulation that he had so carefully built, and she felt cold all over. She started shivering from her very core and felt the nearly convulsive shaking as it made its way to the surface. She felt Ian quickly unbuckling the restraints and knew she had collapsed into his arms, but then she felt herself slide effortlessly into the void again...just like that awful night so many years ago.

* * * *

Sitting in the corner of the master suite watching Callie sleep, Ian was lost in thought when he saw Jace step into the open door. The look on Jace's face spoke volumes—they hadn't caught the woman, and it didn't look like they were going to learn anything from the security tapes either. Sighing heavily he stood and walked to the door. "Tell me you have something. A name, a picture, a description, fuck—*anything* I can tell her when she wakes up."

Jace just shook his head. "I wish I could. God, you have no idea how much I wish I had something we could use. Whoever she was she made a getaway with nearly military precision. She was a guest of Dean White from the State Department. He said he met her yesterday, and since she said she was a member of several of the more popular clubs along the eastern seaboard, he invited her to play with him tonight. We have interviewed him at length, and I get the idea he is telling the truth."

"Until this is resolved, no one brings a guest onto the island for any reason without your or my personal stamp of approval. Check in with Mitch, see if he has anything and ask the Lamonts if their parents are by any chance in the DC area. We could use Daniel's connections, and Catherine has a lot of experience counseling victims with post-traumatic stress disorder, and from what I saw this evening, Callie hit a wall." Ian had caught Callie just before she'd hit the floor at the club and had gotten the soft blanket they kept for aftercare wrapped around her before he felt her muscles go limp, and he knew she had passed out. One of the members in attendance this evening was an emergency room physician, and he'd followed Ian to the club's infirmary and checked Callie for any injuries. Even though her vital signs were fine, the fact that she had awakened only to stare blankly off in to space had been a huge concern. She'd been nearly catatonic for so long it had become frightening.

When he had first decided to start a BDSM club, he'd spent a lot of time at ShadowDance, and one of the things Zach Lamont had been adamant about was that all of his security staff be trained as paramedics and that they have a well-stocked infirmary. Ian was never so grateful for advice as he had been when they'd had plenty of qualified help and all the equipment they had needed close at hand.

Running his hand through his hair in frustration, Ian looked over at the woman sleeping in his bed and said, "I don't know what it is about her, I really don't. But she has gotten to me in a way no one else ever has. Christ, I've had sub's safe word out on me before, but I've never felt as responsible as I did tonight. I tore the blindfold from her eyes the minute I heard the word and 'shattered' is the only word I can use to describe what I saw in her eyes. I don't know what went through her mind so I don't have any clue how to fix it." He looked up at his best friend, and for the first time in years remembered what feeling helpless was like—and he fucking hated it.

"Get our legal team on this right away. And if that rag Callie was working for even thinks about taking this up—dismantle it. And find that bitch." Ian was too frustrated to make decisions, and he knew Jace would pick up the ball and run with it. Ian's focus was going to be on healing the lovely sub who had just started to trust him when she'd had the rug yanked out from under her. He didn't know how he could ever undo the damage that had been done tonight unless she would open up to him. He leaned over and kissed her on the forehead and spoke to her in an emotion-filled whisper. "I'll destroy anyone who hurts you, my pet."

Making his way down the hall toward his office, Ian felt his phone vibrate in his pocket. He smiled when he saw Alex Lamont's name on the ID. Flipping open his phone, he laughed. "That didn't take long."

"Talk to me," was all his friend said. Ian had known Alex and Zach Lamont for most of his life. Their families had gone on vacations together when they were kids. And they had been the only ones he'd confided in when his father had remarried after his mother had died. He'd told them about his new stepmother's attraction to him and all the things she was teaching him. His friends had spent hours trying to get him to see her for what she was, but he'd been so sure it was true love. God, what a fool he'd been.

Their father had also been a great mentor when he had first taken over McGregor Holdings. Ian knew he would have struggled and possibly failed if not for Daniel Lamont's skilled business guidance. Both Daniel and Catherine had made numerous trips back east to spend time with him as he struggled those first few years, and he would be forever in their debt.

Ian quickly explained everything he knew about Callie and Senator Westmore's son. He also recounted the good senator's continued efforts to discredit her. And ended by explaining what had happened this evening. When he'd gotten to his office, they had switched to video-conferencing and included Zach Lamont and Mitch Grayson as well.

Not surprisingly, it was Mitch who offered the first useful piece of information he'd gotten since Callie's meltdown. "You know she probably feels like she's just handed the old bastard exactly what he's been after all these years, right? If your spy took video or pictures, Callie is going to see the damage to her reputation as devastating. That was all she thought she had left. Even though her mother had told her it was her fault, there was that tiny part of her that believed she was still a good girl. If these pictures hit the media, it's really going to hurt her."

Ian's question was the one he knew they were all asking. "Can you stop them? Is there any possibility that you can preempt their release?"

"Not really. But if they release them digitally, they'll leave a footprint, and no matter how faint it is—I'll find them. I'm already on it, I've got several guys here and contacts around the country as well as a couple in Europe watching for them, and we're making a lot of noise about the fact that we're watching. Our hope is, if they know we'll be on their trail, they'll think twice about stepping over that line. If they're going to do it, it'll be quick." Mitch had barely even slowed his typing the whole time he'd been talking.

"Thank you, my friend. I know this is lousy timing for you and I appreciate you taking the time to help. I'm worried you are taking too much time away from Rissa." Ian had no sooner said her name than she stepped in to the frame.

"Ian McGregor, don't you think a thing about that, I may be pregnant, but I'm not a selfish wench…well, not most of the time. As a matter of fact I'd say that for a Weeble, I'm damned reasonable." Rissa smiled when she heard Alex, Zach, and Mitch all groan.

Bryant Davis stepped up and kissed his wife on the check and smiled at Ian. "Ian, nice to speak with you, I wish it was under better circumstances." And then looking at Mitch before returning his focus to Rissa, he said, "I'm going to be the smart husband tonight and not respond to that comment, but I am going to caution our lovely wife about her language. Remember the list, love? We have more paper you know."

Ian nearly laughed out loud at the stricken look on her face and the bright crimson of her blush was plainly visible even through the monitors. But she quickly turned to Ian and said, "You know, Ian, if you think it might help, maybe Kat, Jenna, Tori, and I could do a 'Girls' Night In' party remotely with Callie. We've all been through some pretty nasty shi…stuff, and we'd be happy to help if we can. It's not a perfect plan, but it might do until you all can visit us."

"Thank you, Rissa, you are every bit the princess your husbands say you are. I think you might have a very good idea there, and I'll see about getting that set up if all the men are in agreement. Now, I can tell that Bryant is anxious to get you off your feet, so off to rest you go, sweetness. Take good care of my future godchild." She waved, and Bryant whisked her out of the room quickly.

Alex spoke up first, "Damn, don't any of you repeat this—hell, I'd never hear the end of it, but that really is a good idea. I'll mention it to Katarina as well. I'm sure she'd be happy to make the arrangements, God only knows what kind of decorations and music we'll have to come up with." He laughed, and Ian was happy to see how marriage and parenthood had softened one of the few men who had been more hardened than himself. "Now, Dad and Mom are on their way to DC as we speak, they'll be at your place by noon tomorrow. Dad wants to get closer to the ground so he can connect with a few friends who are likely in the know, and Mom will help with Callie. It doesn't sound like she has ever experienced how healing a mother's love can be, and it won't much matter if she's resistant. Catherine Lamont is fairly persuasive when she sets her mind to something."

Ian laughed when he heard Zach say, "Yeah, like a freight train. Persuasive my ass. When did you get to be such a fucking pussy anyway?" Ian was grateful for his friends, and even though he'd helped them with a number of things over the years, he had never expected anything in return, so their help was truly appreciated. They wrapped up their call quickly with Mitch promising to forward any news as soon as he had it. Mitch had promised him that if there was a chink in either John or Grant Westmore's armor, they'd find it.

Chapter 14

Callie woke up alone in Ian's massive bed feeling like she had been run over by a truck. And her mouth was dry enough she was sure she could cough up dust. Her head was pounding like it had the one and only time she'd ever taken a prescription cough medicine. She had learned the hard way that her body didn't handle medications containing certain narcotics very well. As soon as she tried to stand, she realized her mistake and dropped to her hands and knees as wave upon wave of dizziness swept over her. She didn't know how long she'd been in that position but despite the fact she was starting to get chilled, she was too afraid to move.

"Callie! What the fuck? What happened? Why are you on the floor? Here, let me help you up. Good God, you are ice cold." She heard Ian's voice, but she didn't want to lift her head or the dizziness would return and throwing up would only add to the humiliation she felt over what had happened last night at Club Isola.

"No, please don't move me. I am so dizzy, I'm afraid I'll be sick. I'll be all right in a bit. Please just leave me alone. It's just so embarrassing…please." She could already feel the tears starting to fall, and she really wanted to just curl up in a ball and have a good cry. But she needed to get her shit together and get out of here as soon as possible. Hopefully she could sell enough of what was left in her apartment that she would be able to scrape up enough money to get by until she moved back to Kansas. Her aunt and uncle had always told her she had a home there if she needed it, and she was pretty sure that time had come.

Ian scooped her up, and the dizziness pulled her under and her stomach was heaving as soon as he sat her in front of the toilet. He held her hair and rubbed small circles over the tender skin on her back as she relieved herself of the last vestiges of her dignity. "Pet, what happened? When I left you, you were sleeping so peacefully. I was only gone a few minutes." She could hear the concern in his voice, and she felt bad for worrying him.

He handed her a small glass of water, and she took tiny sips and then rinsed out her mouth. "Oh God, I'm so sorry. I don't really know what's wrong. I am so rarely ill. The only time I'm ever this sick is if I take medication, I have to be very careful. I rarely even take an aspirin. Anything with certain barbiturate properties, according to the doctors, will illicit this response. But I didn't take anything yesterday, I swear it."

Ian picked her up as if she didn't weigh anything at all and settled her on his lap, pulling her against his chest, and just held her tight. "Oh, pet, I'm so very sorry. There was a doctor at the club last night, and after you woke up and were so unresponsive, he gave you a small dose of a tranquilizer to try and get you to rest. We had no idea you couldn't take the medicine. Jesus, it scares the shit out of me to think what might have happened to you." He rocked her gently back and forth for long minutes, and Callie wasn't sure which one of them was more comforted by it. Finally he stood without setting her down, and she let him gently slide her to her feet. "We'll be having company soon, so you need to get in the shower, pet. I'm going to stay right here so I can be sure you're all right. I swear you took ten years off my life when I came through the door." When she opened her mouth to protest, he placed a finger over her lips. "No arguments, you belong to me the rest of the month, remember? And I take very good care of my possessions, pet."

Something about his words saddened her. She had always hoped to find the fairy tale. The prince who would ride in on his white stallion and save her from all of her enemies, but it seemed Ian

McGregor was just going to enjoy a plaything for a month and then she'd be gone. Deciding to put aside her sadness and just do what she needed to do, Callie pulled herself together and moved out of Ian's embrace. As she showered, she promised herself she would work hard to keep her heart out of this whole mess from here on. She couldn't afford to have it broken again, the news about her sister's lies and betrayal had been the final straw. She was tired of being a victim, it was time to "pull herself up by her bootstraps" as her uncle used to tell her. *Okay, Callie, you had your little pity party, now it's time to be a big girl and move on. You can't undo the past, but you can damn well control your future and your attitude. See, Aunt Abbie, I was listening after all.*

* * * *

Ian knew she had immediately started to pull back after his comment—what he didn't know was why. She had already agreed to belong to him for a month, so what was her problem with him referencing what had already been discussed and settled? Suddenly he was very grateful Catherine Lamont was on her way.

Chapter 15

Callie walked into the kitchen after her shower feeling much better—at least she had been until she came face-to-face with several new faces. She stopped just before crossing the threshold and considered returning to the safety of the master suite despite the fact she was starving. Damn her loud, growling stomach anyway, it had given her away before she had a chance to retreat. The stunningly beautiful woman who Callie guessed to be in her forties or maybe her early fifties looked up, and a smile lit up her entire face.

"Oh, there you are, come on in here and get something in your stomach, dear. I'm Catherine Lamont, and this lovely lady preparing our luncheon feast is Inez, Ian's housekeeper extraordinaire. She is a treasure and grossly underappreciated I am sure." There was just something about the woman that immediately put Callie at ease. Even though she looked like a runway model, she seemed very down to earth and genuine.

The large man sitting nearby spoke up just then, "Don't be making trouble, my love, or you'll get us both thrown out into the bay." He turned to Callie and smiled before saying, "It's nice to meet you, Callie. I'm Daniel Lamont, and I believe you have already met a friend of ours, Mitch Grayson." Something about Daniel Lamont seemed so familiar, but she couldn't get her mind to grasp onto whatever it was. It wasn't his looks or his name, she was sure she would remember those, it was more about his *presence*. Suddenly she made the connection, Daniel Lamont was a Dom. It seemed odd that she suddenly seemed to be surrounded by them. Was she just now noticing that personality type or was she just now recognizing the men she met for who and what they were? She couldn't help wondering if she'd met a lot of Dominants over the years and just hadn't realized it or maybe it was that Doms tended to stick together—like a flock or something? She gave herself a mental slap for her absurdity then started thinking about what a great angle it would be for her story. Then the realization that she wouldn't be writing the story after all slammed into her. The depressing reality of what had happened last night brought her back to the present and with it all the details of that unpleasant memory.

Realizing that Daniel had moved to stand directly in front of her, she automatically dropped her gaze to the floor. She felt his finger under her chin and looked up at his urging. His words surprised her. "I see the same sadness in your eyes that I saw in our daughter Jenna's eyes years ago. I made a huge mistake when I let her hide the truth—a mistake she paid dearly for—for far too long. I won't let Ian make that same mistake, I promise you."

When Callie looked over at Catherine Lamont, there were tears in her eyes, a fact that her husband hadn't missed either. Callie watched as he pulled his sweet wife into his arms and gave her a comforting hug before swatting her ass and grinning. "When's lunch, love? I'm starving."

Just as they were sitting down to eat, Ian and Jace walked into the room. Both men leaned down to ask her how she was feeling before sitting on either side of her. Thanks to Catherine's bubbly presence, Callie felt more at ease and it didn't seem so obvious that she wasn't really participating in the conversation. She'd tried to surreptitiously look out the window toward the small boat dock. She was trying to see if her small rowboat was still tied there. Ian leaned over and placed his hand over hers, stilling the fingers she hadn't even realized she was tapping nervously. "It's no longer there, pet. Jace had it returned several days ago, and your deposit is with your belongings. Stop fidgeting. And don't even think about leaving this island without my permission." When she looked at him openmouthed and wide eyed, he laughed out loud. "Don't look so shocked, pet. It was written all over your lovely face."

After lunch the men excused themselves to Ian's office, pleading business, which left Callie in limbo. Catherine looked over at her and smiled. "I asked Jace to leave us a golf cart so we can go exploring. I do my best thinking when I'm moving. Come on, let's go play."

Callie learned quickly that Catherine Lamont was not a woman who was easy to ignore. She also discovered that the woman's gorgeous body and face hid a wicked sense of humor and a Mensa-worthy IQ.

Late in the afternoon as they sat dangling their bare feet over the edge of the dock, Catherine told Callie about why they had started the domestic violence and sexual assault centers they founded in Denver. How they had found a young, badly abused immigrant cowering in an alley one night and how that woman had become a member of their family for all intents and purposes. Callie had laughed until she'd cried at Catherine's stories about how Selita managed to completely butcher common American slang. But it had been the story about her daughter's rape that had touched Callie's heart. The monster who had raped the young woman was a member of the Lamont brothers' Special Forces team and had used Jenna's love for her brothers to keep her silent. He'd assured Jenna that her brothers would not make it home from their next mission if she told anyone what had happened. The madman had returned recently to silence her once and for all, but he'd come up against a very different woman this time. Callie's tears of empathy and compassion for Jenna had been replaced by admiration at how she had trained tirelessly in self-defense so she'd never be a victim again. Jenna Lamont had even competed at the collegiate level and had beaten most of her brother's fellow teammates before word had spread and they all but quit sparring with her.

Callie had tilted her head back and was laughing when she heard what sounded like a firecracker and then felt air rush by just in front of her chin. Catherine had grabbed her and thrown them both in the water just as she heard another shot and the roar of a boat motor a split second before she'd gone under the water.

When both of them surfaced, Catherine had grabbed her and asked, "Are you all right? Can you swim?" Callie had only managed to nod quickly when Catherine pulled her close. "Hang on to my shirt and stay under the water as long as you can. I know the men will be here soon." They ducked under the water and moved so they were under the planking of the dock. By the time they surfaced the second time, Ian and Daniel were shouting their names. Callie was still too stunned to respond, but thank God Catherine had her wits about her. "Down here, Daniel. We're both fine, but we'd sure appreciate getting out of this water. Damn, I just had my hair done, too." She looked at Callie and winked. Callie shook her head, Catherine Lamont was the second-best thing that had happened to her in a very long time.

* * * *

While they waited for the women to finish dressing, Ian and Daniel met with Jace and several other members of the security team. They'd reviewed the tapes and forwarded the images of the boat to the local Coast Guard station. Of course the registration numbers on the side of the boat and the name on the back had been covered so it was unlikely they'd ever be able to get a positive identification of the vessel. Daniel had already called Alex and Zach, and no one doubted all the resources of the Lamonts were fully in motion. Ian didn't imagine either man had taken the news very well that their mother had been in the line of fire.

When Ian heard doors opening and closing upstairs, he moved into the hall just in time to see Catherine emerge from the guest suite and join Callie. "Well, I don't know about you, but that's the most excitement I've had in a very long time. You, my dear, are a very interesting person to, as the girls would say, 'hang out with.'"

Catherine looked like she was enjoying all the excitement, but Ian could tell Callie had been deeply shaken by the incident.

Seeing Callie's eyes fill up with tears and her entire body start to shake, he moved quickly to her and wrapped her in his warm embrace. Catherine looked up mortified at Callie's distress. "Oh my, I didn't mean to make her feel badly about what happened. I just wanted you to know we are with you on this thing."

Callie pulled back and smiled at her. "I'm just sorry that I've brought trouble here. And I sure don't want someone else getting hurt because of me."

"Oh posh...I meant what I said. I never get to see any of the action. The girls back at ShadowDance have had all kinds of adventures, and I feel like a stick in the mud. But, now? Oh, sister, now I have a great story to tell at the next girls' night in 'rita party." She giggled, and Callie had to laugh at her new friend's outlook.

As they all sat around Ian's office discussing this afternoon's events, Mitch Grayson called and asked to be put on the video feed. "I think I might have something for you. I used the face recognition software I've been working on and think I may have a possible on the woman at the club." Looking at Callie, he asked, "Do you know a woman by the name of Trish Simmons?"

Ian watched as Callie paled visibly. "Yes, she was Charlie Ives's girlfriend in high school. I thought I heard they'd gotten married, but I'm not sure about that."

"They did indeed get married. And it seems good ole Charlie left Trish with a lot of debt when he died a few months ago. And oddly enough, she was recently offered a job in Senator Westmore's office. And according to recent banking records, her debt seems to be mysteriously dwindling, and she has become good friends with Nanette Westmore."

Daniel Lamont spoke up, saying, "This is enough to launch an investigation into where her money is suddenly coming from since she is now on the federal payroll. I'll get the ball rolling on that,

Catherine and I are heading into DC tonight for dinner with friends. It just so happens one of those is the head of the Ethics Committee and he is no fan of Senator Westmore's, I assure you. Hopefully we'll be able to stir up enough smoke that he'll be busy covering his ass and he'll forget about Callie. I'm sure he'll have someone he needs to groom for the big toss under the bus."

"Well, if they can't find the money trail, they aren't looking because I found it and have it all documented. All of the deposits lead right back to the senator's Chief of Staff, Carl Remley. Let them know you have access to the information, that will probably motivate them." Mitch smiled as if he'd just found the keys to the kingdom.

"Oh, indeed it will. They hate it when I know something they don't. Damn I do appreciate what you do, Mitch. I swear if it wouldn't piss my boys off so much, I'd get you transferred into something a bit more profitable." Daniel Lamont had all but retired, but he loved keeping his fingers in the pie just enough to make Alex crazy and everybody knew it. He had also stepped up to take a larger role in Lamont Oil since his daughter had gotten married and was expecting her first child in a few months. "Now, when is that beautiful wife of yours going to bless us with our *bonus* grandchild?"

Everyone could hear Rissa yell from the background, "My water just broke so we're waiting for Mitch so we can head down the mountain, Sir." Callie wasn't sure who was the most shocked, Daniel or Mitch.

Poor Mitch seemed genuinely flustered. "Oh shit. Oh, I mean shoot. I have to go. I'll keep you all posted. Bye." And they were all left staring at a black screen.

Chapter 16

Daniel and Catherine Lamont had been gone for three days, and Ian had to admit the house had seemed awfully quiet. And then Ian had been wrapped up in a couple of business meetings in New York and had been gone for the past day and half. He'd asked Jace to make sure Callie was safe, but he didn't want her to have internet access yet. He'd explained that he would be gone and that he would call and check in with her several times a day, and she had yet to answer a call. He was damned tired of talking to Jace and Inez. Their reports were that she rarely left her room except to jog along the trails of the island and to retrieve books from the small library next to Ian's office. Dee Tate had gotten her to agree to come back to the Club on Saturday night since she and Mike would be doing a scene.

Ian and Jace always circled the island before landing as a security precaution, so he'd seen Callie standing out on the beach looking off toward land. As soon as he got to the house, he shed his jacket, tie, and shoes and headed her direction. He wasn't sure she had heard him walk up behind her and that inattention to her own safety concerned him. He wrapped his arms around her from behind and pulled her back against his chest. "I missed you, pet."

"Oh, God, Ian, you scared me. I didn't hear you. When did you get back? I didn't see a boat come over." She sounded disconnected and sad.

"Well, we flew the helicopter right over you, sweetness. I have to tell you, I'm not that pleased to know you are so distracted that you didn't even hear us. Now, suppose you tell me what has your mind all tied in knots."

She took so long to answer he wasn't sure she was going to, but then she took a deep breath and confessed, "I was just wondering what is to become of me. I obviously can't ever go back to the job I had. I'm sure all my possessions are gone by now. A few days ago I was planning to just head back to my aunt and uncle's in Kansas. They said I could always come home. But now, I know that I need to stay for the whole month. I have always prided myself on not breaking a promise or my word...so that means I need to stay. But...well, it has to be different from now on, Ian. My heart won't take any more damage right now. I know that, and I'm going to protect it, I hope you'll understand."

Ian was stunned by her honesty. He'd never known a woman as brave as the one he held loosely in his arms at that moment. He leaned down and nipped at the sensitive spot on her shoulder that he knew was a hot spot for her and smiled when he heard her soft groan. "Well, pet, I'm glad you have decided to stay for the entire month, because I had no intention of letting you go easily. I do understand your need to protect your heart, and I am not sure I can be the man you deserve, but I'd like to think we can enjoy each other for the time we have left, and perhaps we'll find the answers we both seek."

As he'd been talking, he'd been slowly moving her toward a large rock that most people didn't even notice sitting right in the center of the beach. The rock had been flattened on top, and it was exactly the height for either he or Jace to bend a sub over and fuck them. And even though Ian knew Jace had used it several times, Ian just hadn't found the right woman—until Callie.

"Now, I'd like to talk to you about the fact that I told you I would be calling several times each day to check in and you did not take one of those calls. Just so you know I was counting, I made twelve calls and you'll get two strokes for each of those that you did not answer. Plus the six you're getting for not being more aware of your surroundings and taking better precautions with your safety.

Remember, your safety is my chief concern. I will insist that you take it as seriously as I do."

He still had his arms wrapped around her from the back, and he could feel her heart pounding and that her respiration had gotten more rapid and shallow. Leaning down so that he was speaking directly in to her ear, he whispered. "I'm going to punish you for not taking my calls. That is not, nor will it ever be acceptable, pet. You will *always* and I do mean always take my calls immediately, do I make myself clear?"

"Yes." He just waited the long seconds it took for her to realize her error and to answer correctly. "Yes, Sir. I understand." God, he loved the breathless sound of her voice as she slid into a submissive state of mind. He had never wanted a 24/7 slave before. Hell, he'd never used the same sub more than a handful of times so that they didn't ever have an opportunity to get the wrong idea. And usually by the time he'd spent as much time with them as he had with Callie the first day they'd met, he was trying to figure out how to get away from them. But with Callie, he was trying to figure out all the ways he could keep her close.

"Remove your shorts, pet. Hand them to me." He released her and turned her so that she stood facing him. As she unsnapped the short shorts and slid them down her legs, he felt all the breath leave his lungs. The moonlight illuminated the white lace panties she was *almost* wearing, making them almost luminescent. "Now those beautiful lace panties. And I will remind you that you are not to wear panties unless I have specifically given them to you. You'll get two extra swats for that, pet. I believe that brings your total up to thirty-two. That is an awful lot for one session, so I believe I'll divide it up a bit. You'll get half tonight and the other half tomorrow night during a little get-together I've planned."

He heard her soft gasp but she didn't argue. When he slipped his fingers between her legs he found that she was soaking wet. Her arousal was nearly dripping off his hand. "Oh, I do believe you like the idea of getting a spanking in front of our friends. Don't you, pet? You are already wondering how I'll do it aren't you? Will I lay you over my lap and pull up the sheer dress I've bought for you to wear? Or perhaps I'll strip you and make you assume the punishment pose in the middle of the room so that the other Doms and subs can see that beautifully smooth pussy of yours. Or then again, maybe I'll make you spend the entire evening naked and let each of the Doms have a few of the swats for themselves. I won't let them fuck what's mine, but I'm not opposed to sharing your punishment if I think it will help reinforce the lesson. Something to consider the next time you deliberately ignore my attempts to speak with you."

She had continued to pant her breaths, and her pussy was so wet he was enjoying the sound his fingers were making as they slid back and forth. He had fucked her with his fingers several times, and the slurping sound had almost been enough to make him blow his load in his trousers. "Turn around and spread your legs apart, pet. I'm going to give you sixteen swats and then I'm going to fuck you before I take you back to the house. Jace is meeting us in a bit, we'll be introducing you to something new tonight." She had her legs spread, and he bent her at the waist so that she lay against the cool rock. "That rock is cold isn't it? It's going to make your nipples rock hard and keep them that way so that I can pinch them at my leisure." Sliding his hand between her breast and the rock, he pinched first one and the other nipple until he heard her gasp. "I'm going to see these clamped tomorrow night. I bought you some beautiful clamps with lovely stones that match your eyes. They will be lovely underneath your dress. Everyone will be able to see the gift your Master has given you. Now, we begin."

Ian administered her spanking in a random pattern and changed the timing and intensity of the strokes so that she wasn't able to anticipate where or when the next stroke would come. He knew she was floating in sub-space and was thrilled she was able to reach that level of endorphin-induced euphoria so easily. He didn't doubt for a minute she was still going to be sporting some of the marks tomorrow night, but that would work in his favor when all the other Doms sprouted wood the minute they walked in to the party. There was nothing like a few remnants of a punishment to get a Dom's blood pumping straight to his cock. What Callie didn't know was that tomorrow night's guests had been selected for very special reasons. Each of the five Doms was an expert in some type of play, and the two subs who were attending would do exactly as they were told without hesitation, so they would be great role models for her. And he planned to make her punishment a very large part of an evening she was not going to ever forget.

He had managed to lower his pants so that as soon as he landed the last swat he slid into her wet heat in one smooth stroke and commanded her to "Come, my pet. Let your Master hear you shout your pleasure as your beautiful cunt milks the cum from my cock and balls."

Callie screamed, and he felt the immediate pulsing of her internal muscles as they clenched around him in a rapid fire sequence that had him straining to maintain control. *Jesus Christ, she is going to squeeze my dick completely off. I've never felt anything like this woman. Her pussy feels like hot, wet velvet.* He waited until she was beginning to come back down from her release, and then he started fucking her in long strokes, slamming all the way in so that the head of his cock was bumping against her cervix. And when he knew he was close to coming, he tilted his pelvis so that his cock slammed into her G-spot as he shouted to her, "Come again, Callie. Come again for your Master."

She went right back over the edge, and this time she took him with her. He felt as though his balls were being turned inside out—his soul being pulled from his body with each pulsing jet of cum he sent into her body. He'd never had sex without a condom before Callie, and he felt a primal satisfaction knowing he had marked her with his seed.

He lay over her back as he tried to catch his breath, and felt the heat of her paddled ass against his groin. "Master Jace is going to see your red ass and know you've received part of your punishment. And we're going to walk back up to the house now. My seed is going to run down the insides of your legs, and you're going to leave it exactly where it is. I want to see my marks on you and that includes the seed. When we get to the bedroom, you'll stand in the corner with your legs spread shoulder width apart while I take my shower. Now, let's get moving. I'm anxious for the next part of our evening. I've been looking forward to this since the first moment I laid eyes on you."

Chapter 17

Jace had entered the master suite not long after Ian had led Callie inside. He was sure she didn't know he'd watched and heard their entire scene outside on the beach. There wasn't a spot on the island that wasn't covered by security cameras and most of those had audio capabilities as well as sensitive night-vision lenses. He sat in the lounge chair and just watched Callie for long seconds before speaking to her. "Your ass is a lovely shade of red, sweetness. I see your Master has discussed his displeasure with you for not answering his calls. And I see he let you stand here with his seed trailing down your legs so that you would have good reason to remember who you belong to. It's difficult to forget that you belong to a man when he leaves his mark on you isn't it?"

"Yes, Sir. I'm very sorry for not taking his calls. I just couldn't…it well, it hurt too much after what he said before he left. I just had to, well, I had to step back a bit, you know?" Jace knew that she had shut Ian out before he left for the business trip, and he also knew that Ian wasn't entirely sure why.

Jace saw Ian step out of the shower and signaled him to stay silent. Perhaps he could coax a little information from the tiny beauty who had captured his friend's heart. "What did your Master say that put that pain in your heart, sweetness?" His tone was soft but wouldn't leave any doubt but that he expected a truthful answer. When she seemed to hesitate, he cautioned, "Your ass looks awfully sore, Callie. I doubt you want me adding to your punishment tonight, so I suggest you answer me."

He could practically hear her mind working to figure out how to answer without really answering. But he'd read enough of her background information to know that, in the end, she wouldn't be able to lie to him.

"Well, I was sort of...well, getting kind of caught up in him, if you know what I mean. I know it was foolish to think that a smart, good-looking guy like him would be interested in someone plain like me. And well, when he reminded me that I'm only going to be here for a month, well, it brought me crashing back to earth." Jace could see her small frame shaking from her silent sobs, and he'd have liked nothing more than to pull her in to his arms and comfort her, but he was sure he hadn't gotten it all yet. But he did find it very interesting that she had mentioned Ian's intelligence and good looks, but hadn't mentioned the fact the man was a billionaire. *Yes, indeed. Amazing young woman, this Callie Reece. And I can hardly wait to bring her pissant sister to heel for all the pain she has caused this sweet soul.*

"I'm curious, Callie—tell me why you don't think Ian could be interested in you. Did he say that? Or has someone else convinced you that you aren't worthy of everything your heart desires? Because if that's the case, I know that Master Ian and I would both enjoy spending a little quality time alone with that person."

This time she didn't answer, she just wrapped her arms around herself and put her feet together as if she was trying to make herself smaller, as if smaller could be equated with invisible. Hell, it was probably exactly what she'd been trying to do ever since she'd been raped and her wicked mother had all but thrown her to the wolves. Jace knew that the woman would never get another shot at Callie if he or Ian had anything to say about it. Ian McGregor was not a man anyone wanted to fuck with, that was for sure. And even though Callie would always belong to Ian, she would hold a very special place in his heart as well.

Ian had moved in to the room and mouthed his thanks before wrapping his arms around his sobbing sub. "That's enough of that for tonight. We'll talk about his more later, but so that your mind can put this aside tonight, I want you to know that I referred to our time together as a month because I wasn't sure you were ready to hear anything else yet. And truthfully I wasn't sure I was ready either. But I have some options I want to discuss with you in a few days. I have a couple of ideas that I think might interest you very much—that is if you'd be interested in staying on the island and supervising a project I'm planning." Jace watched as his friend's touch and voice seemed to magically soothe her soul. Having known Ian for many years, Jace was thrilled to see the way these two wounded souls seemed to be healing each other. He'd help them and then hope like hell he found his own soul partner in the near future.

Jace spoke up then, "Come along, sweetness, you and I are going to take a quick shower while your Master sets up a few things in here. Let's get cleaned up so we can play a bit more before we put you to bed." Ian turned her into his arms, and Jace led her into the bath where he removed her shirt and lacy bra before removing his own sweatpants. They didn't spend a lot of time in the shower, he made sure she was clean and relaxed before he finished his own shower and toweled them both dry. "Lean over the counter, Callie, I want to insert this in your anus now so it begins to work before we move into the other room." He watched her eyes go wide before she slowly leaned over the counter. He spread her ass cheeks and pushed a small syringe full of a topical numbing lubricant just inside her pretty little rosette. It would help them stretch her without any unnecessary pain, they were both large men and he wanted her first experience with double penetration to be as pleasant as possible. He also rubbed some soothing aloe gel into her bruised ass and then led her in to the bedroom. Leaning close, he whispered, "Relax and enjoy, sweetness. Let us take you to a whole new level of pleasure."

Chapter 18

When he had first approached her outside on the beach, Callie hadn't meant to tell Ian so much detail about her thoughts, but his voice and touch seduced her easily. She'd had a lot of time to read while he had been gone, and his library had yielded several great books about the psychological implications of the various elements of BDSM. Several of the authors had explained the dynamics and the concept of *total power exchange*. She had been surprised at how wrong her first impression of the term had been. The explanation had made perfect sense once she'd given it consideration. What she didn't understand was how she would ever be able to trust someone that much. Everything she'd read about a submissive placing him or herself into the Dominant's care had sounded like some kind of fairy tale, and she'd let go of that fantasy a long time ago.

If she was to be honest with herself, it wasn't the rape itself which was the most painful part of her past. The most damage to her trust had come from her mother's reaction to the trauma Callie had experienced. Her mother's callous treatment had caused her to feel like she was somehow to blame for not only what had happened to her, but that she was also responsible for the decline of her mother's social position. In truth, it was her continued victimization at the hands of the one person who was supposed to love her unconditionally that had been the far greatest source of pain.

She and Catherine had discussed her mother's actions briefly. Catherine had assured her that while her mother's actions were completely unacceptable, they weren't unprecedented. And that after working with victims for over twenty years, she was still seeing new ways people could revictimize those who were already suffering. Catherine also assured her that it was her mother's problem and that allowing those old hurts to continue holding her back was self-defeating. Callie's only problem was convincing her heart to listen to her head.

Feeling Ian's hands moving over her skin and his warm breath against her ear had brought her back to the present. She wanted to trust him because there was something about him that called to her. It was as if his soul understood how hers felt. The deepest part of him seemed to know what it felt like to experience the pain that only a loved one can inflict. Was it possible that his spirit was as much in need of healing as her own? Could they actually help heal each other?

When Ian had started talking about the punishment she was going to get for not taking his calls, she'd felt the moisture rush through her pussy. She'd remembered the book she had read yesterday that had explained the connection between pain and pleasure. The words had seemed to jump off the page at her, and for the first time in her life she'd wished she had a way to ask the author for more information.

The first swats had hurt—*a lot*—but then need and arousal had swamped her, and even though she was crying there had been something cleansing about the whole experience. It felt like someone had uncoiled a spring, and all its tension had been released. And when he'd said he was going to finish her punishment tomorrow in front of their dinner party guests, her knees had grown so weak she'd barely been able to remain standing. He taunted her with possibilities, and she'd felt as if her heart was finally beginning to grasp the basics of BDSM's appeal for so many people. Reading about it had helped, but it was the actual experience that was bringing it to life.

Callie hadn't even realized Ian had lowered his trousers until he slammed his cock into her. She'd been completely lost in the sensations of pain turned to fire that raced up and then back down her spine like lightning until it settled directly in her aching clit. When his cock pushed into her, she felt each ridge pass over tissues engorged with blood. His flesh felt like it was on fire, and the added heat only heightened her desire.

All she remembered was that he'd demanded that she come and she had complied. She knew her wail would carry across the water, but it didn't matter because her Master had ordered it. She knew the colors she'd flown through had been spectacular and that she had been left gasping in an attempt to replace the oxygen her brain had missed out on during her trip down the orgasmic super-highway. How she'd gotten back to the master suite was a mystery.

Ian had made her stand in the corner with her legs apart and forbidden her to clean his seed from her legs. It had been both humiliating and embarrassing until she'd just accepted that it was what pleased her Master so there was no reason for her to think about it any further. She'd heard Jace enter, and it had sounded as if he'd sat down behind her. When he'd started asking her questions she had silently cursed her truthfulness. At times like this she really wished she was able to lie. She didn't remember exactly what he'd asked or how she had replied, she only remembered thinking that she'd said too much. And she had wondered if endorphins doubled as truth serum as well as what her A & P professor had called "the brain's own morphine."

After her shower with Jace, he'd put something into her anus that had caused a hot flash of warm sensation then it had seemed to go almost numb. Jace had also rubbed her stinging ass cheeks with a gel that had taken away almost all of the burning. When she had started to comb through her tangled hair, he'd taken the comb and meticulously worked from the ends to her scalp, taking great care to not pull or break her hair before separating it and braiding it so that it fell down her back. "I don't think either Master Ian or I can wait until your hair dries to sink into you, sweetness," was all he'd said before leading her back in to the bedroom.

Callie gasped as they walked through the doorway and she saw how Ian had transformed the room. There were candles everywhere. It looked as if every available flat surface had been utilized, and the effect was enchanting. Ian held his hand out to her, and she automatically moved to stand in front of him. "Don't look so surprised, pet. Doms can be romantic bastards, too. And I assure you, the look on your face as you took in my meager attempts made it very worthwhile." His smile melted her resolve, and just like that, all her best intentions to keep her heart safe melted like the wax around a wick.

* * * *

Ian didn't know what had prompted him to fill the room with candles, it had just seemed like the thing to do, and one look at Callie's expression had made it all worth his trouble. He hadn't missed Jace's raised eyebrow either. No doubt but that he'd be answering his best friend's queries later. But at least for the moment, he was free to enjoy the benefits of a happy sub.

"We have very special plans for you tonight, pet. And those plans do not include any more punishment—as long as you're a good girl and follow instructions—the rest of tonight is all about your pleasure." Jace had moved around them and was placing the items they'd be using close at hand. Neither of them liked having to stop in the middle of a scene to retrieve a toy or lube, so they prided themselves on being well prepared. Breaks in the flow when playing with a new sub were particularly distracting, and Callie was still insecure enough they neither one wanted her to have any reason to become distracted.

Watching her closely as he moved her closer to the open doors leading to the small terrace, he smiled when her breathing hitched and the violet in her eyes deepened to a lovely purple. "I want to start outside, pet. There will be security patrols passing by soon, and I'm looking forward to giving them a bit of a show to whet their appetites for tomorrow night." He knew that both Gage Hughes and Logan

Douglas were on duty tonight and would be making perimeter sweeps around the house in a few minutes. Ian had called them while Jace and Callie showered to make sure everything was set up and the timing was going to work out. Both Doms had agreed to attend the small get-together tomorrow night, and Ian looked forward to easing Callie back into public play. Each of the Doms he'd invited to the party had a very specific specialty that they'd be using to both punish and pleasure his sweet sub.

The terrace was lined with tiny fairy lights, and with the candlelight spilling out from the bedroom, the setting was perfect. The blonde shades of Callie's hair shimmered in the low light, and her lightly tanned skin was practically glowing. Jace had positioned a large pillow on the ground, and Ian nodded to it before saying, "Kneel for your Master, pet. I want to feel your mouth surrounding my cock. Use your tongue and mouth only, keep your hands behind your back." As she lowered herself gracefully into position, he smiled. "Very pretty, pet. Have you been practicing?" When she nodded, he leaned down and kissed her forehead. "Such a good girl, that pleases me very much."

He could tell his words had struck a chord with her, and he suddenly realized the tiny beauty before him had very little experience with praise. That was one thing he was looking forward to changing—soon. Moving to stand in front of her, he watched as her eyes moved over him, and he felt her gaze as if she'd actually touched him. His cock was already aching and ready for release despite the sound fucking he'd given her on the beach. Pushing his cock close, he traced the smooth head over her plump lips slowly as he asked her quietly, "Pet, do you have any experience with pleasuring a man with your mouth beyond Master Jace?" He watched as she slowly shook her head from side to side, her eyes never leaving the throbbing purple head.

When her eyes filled with unshed tears, she murmured, "No, I'm sorry. But I want very much to please you, will you teach me?"

"Oh, baby, it will be a pleasure. Eyes on mine, pet." With that he started slowly pushing past her lips, gently thrusting, gaining a bit of depth with each move. "Breathe through your nose. That's it. Now, relax your lower jaw a bit more. The tension you had before will be wonderful at another time, but right now, I'm too close, and it felt much too good." He saw the relief in her eyes and was pleased he'd explained why he'd needed her to back off a bit. "Now I'm going to push in a bit further. Remember to breathe through your nose." He pushed in further with each thrust until he was all the way to the top of her throat. "Jesus Christ, pet, that feels incredible. You are not going to need much guidance on blow jobs, you are a natural. The fact that you apparently have no gag reflex is an incredible gift to your Master."

He thrust in several more times, each time going down her tight throat until his balls were against her chin. Finally pulling out so that he didn't fall over the edge that he was skating dangerously close to, he took a minute to catch his breath, leaning back and smiling at her. He finally looked up at Jace. "You have to come over here and see what our sweet girl can do. Her mouth is devil-blessed, that is for sure."

Jace's cock was just as long as Ian's and probably even thicker, but Ian watched as she easily deep-throated him as well. Ian had to suppress his smile, Jace hadn't had the quickie down on the beach, so Ian knew his friend was really struggling to maintain his control. "Holy fuck, she is incredible. Her tongue touches each of the sensitive spots without any direction from me, and that throat of hers is so tight. Oh shit, sweetness, I have to pull out or I'm going to shoot my seed down your throat, and that is not what we'd planned for tonight. But I'm going to make sure I get that opportunity in the very near future." Jace looked up at Ian and mouthed "lucky bastard" before moving around behind Callie.

Ian held out his hand and helped her stand. He knew the instant she became aware of the two men standing just at the edge of the shadows watching them, and he was deeply gratified that she immediately sought out his gaze as if seeking his approval. Stepping forward, he leaned down and spoke close to her ear. "Thank you for looking to your Master for guidance, that is exactly as it should be. They are here by my invitation, and as you can see, they're enjoying it very much." Both men were standing in a typical Dom stance, but they had positioned themselves so that their erections were clearly visible as they pushed incessantly against their denim jeans. "Do you see how you have turned them on, my pet? I'm sure they are even more anxious for tomorrow night's little get-together after seeing you taking our cocks clear to the root. Now, we want to begin preparing that beautiful ass of yours, so bend over this raised bench, that's it, perfect."

They had moved a narrow, padded-top bench from the playroom so they would be able to enjoy the moonlight and the audience before moving Callie back inside. She lay over the bench, and he moved her feet wider apart and then stepped back so Jace could insert the plug they were going to use to stretch her rear entrance. As Jace began lubing her, Ian stepped further in front of her so she could see him without straining her neck. "Listen to everything Master Jace says to you, pet. Follow his instructions to the letter. He is something of an expert in this particular area of BDSM play. He knows more about the anal regions of subs than anyone has a right to know." He heard whispered words of agreement from the men watching and had to smile when Jace glared at all three of them.

Jace leaned over Callie. "They are just jealous, sweetness. I seem to have a way of getting the best results when it comes to this type of penetration. I promise you that I'm going to make sure this is an experience you'll be begging to repeat—often." Ian heard Callie gasp as Jace penetrated her ass with his fingers. And he watched as Jace worked his magic, quickly eliciting soft moans from her. She was pushing back against his fingers and lifting her ass into the thrusts. "Oh, sweetness, you like having my fingers fucking your beautiful ass, don't you? Feel how you are moving into the strokes." Ian could see that with his next forward thrust Jace had pushed in with two fingers. He wouldn't have even been sure she had noted the change if it hadn't been for the deeper arch of her back and the low moan of pleasure she had made just before she had started to tremble. When Jace stilled his movements, Ian heard her soft whine. "Not yet, sweetie, we don't want you to come yet. But I can't tell you how pleased we are that you are enjoying yourself so much that you want to." No doubt Callie would have been able to hear to praise in Jace's words of caution.

Ian had seen her close her eyes, lost in the pleasure, and hadn't bothered to correct her because he'd been anxious for her to connect anal play with pleasure, but now it was time to pull her back from the edge. "Open our eyes, pet. Keep your eyes on mine. I want to be able to see your pleasure as Master Jace stretches your tight little ass muscles. I want you to think about how full you are going to feel with him fucking your ass as I fuck your sweet pussy again." He could see she was struggling to keep her eyes focused on his as she became more and more immersed in the pleasure.

Each time she was just a breath away from release, Jace slowed his pace or shifted just enough that he was able to bring her back, and Ian knew she was very near the point of no return. They wanted her near the peak, but not so frustrated that she gave up chasing the release her body had been seeking. Ian nodded to Jace and then watched as the man fully seated the plug and then pulled Callie back up to standing. Watching as she worked to regain her equilibrium, Ian nodded to the two men watching. "We'll look forward to seeing you tomorrow evening, gentlemen. Thank you for your time, and if you have any questions about tomorrow, don't hesitate to give me a call—tomorrow."

Chapter 19

Ian watched as Jace carried Callie back in to the bedroom. He could hear him whispering to her. "Just let us take care of you. Follow our directions and this is going to rock your world, sweetness. When your Master comes in, he's going to lie on this lounger. But before we begin, I'm going to make sure that luscious pussy of yours is all wet with your sweet juices. This is also going to be a new position for you. We'll call this 'present.' Up on the bed, you go. Now, on your knees, but instead of your hands, put your forearms on the bed. Perfect, now arch your back and spread those beautiful legs wide."

Ian stood in the doorway watching as Jace taught Callie one of their favorite positions for subs. The "present" position was the perfect mix of display and submission in Ian's opinion. Every fold was opened up like the soft petals of a summer rose, displaying the treasure within. Ian could see Callie falling under the spell of Jace's gentle touch. It was clear that she was extremely responsive to both sides of BDSM play. She craved the dominance and control, but she had also felt the pleasure-pain connection quickly each time they'd used it with her.

But the tiny beauty seemed to respond equally to touch that was pure seduction also, and that pleased Ian more than he was willing to admit. Even though he had a reputation as one of the darker Doms around, it wasn't an entirely accurate description. He'd just found it convenient to hide behind that image. He used it as a shield against woman who would have pursued him for money or connections. Most of the women he met were society leeches or social-climbing bimbos, and it was easy to let his reputation filter out a lot of woman who were only interested in one kind of power exchange—the sort where his power became their own. He had found it easier to keep his sexual encounters framed within very strictly structured and negotiated scenes inside Club Isola. Hell, his personal playroom had yet to even be used. He'd begun to think it had been a huge waste of time and money—until Callie rowed herself into his life. Callie Reece was the first woman he'd actually considered building a future with since he'd been a teenager with delusional dreams perpetrated by the sexual predator his father had married.

He smiled as he watched Callie begin to move as if her body was following music only she could hear. *Ah, my sweet sub, the dance of submission begins.* He finally spoke up, "Make her tell us how she feels. I want to make certain she is aware of exactly what her body is feeling."

When she didn't respond immediately, Jace asked, "Did you hear Master Ian, sweetness? Best give him what he's asked for."

"Yes, Sir. I heard him...I was just trying to find the words to describe the feelings...and it is hard to describe what's happening with my body when my thoughts feel like the soft mist that falls from a heavy fog on a spring morning." Ian loved the breathy quality of her voice and the picture she had painted with words that had told him more than she knew. Suddenly he couldn't wait to take her to visit his father's homeland. She had just told him how much she'd enjoy that trip.

"Well, pet, let's try this. I'll ask you direct questions. Let's see if that works better for you." Ian let his voice drop deeper in timbre and cadence as he fought for his own control as well as hers.

"Oh, yes, please. I think, oh well...um, I think I can do that...maybe...probably. I'll try, oh God, it feels so good, I can barely think straight." Ian looked up at Jace and nearly laughed out loud at his friend's cocky grin. Ian knew full well that Jace Garrett had the skills to bring almost any woman to climax within seconds. He could also leave a woman on the edge of release for hours, and right now he was clearly enjoying the process.

"Pet, I want you to describe what Master Jace's fingers are doing." Even he could hear the roughness of his voice. He wasn't going to be able to stall very much longer, he wanted her too badly.

"His fingers are making me so...oh, so...it's like my whole body is lighting up on the inside. And I can't think of anything but what it's going to feel like to have both of you inside me at the same time. Oh, please."

Jace leaned over her. "Please what, sweetness? What do you need?" Ian had already moved the narrow lounger. He was going to burst if he didn't get inside her sweet cunt right away. Jesus, who was he kidding? He was likely to burst just from the sweet sensation of sinking into her. Jace picked her up easily and moved her to where Ian lay back, waiting. "Step over him and sink him into your pussy, sweetness. We are going to double fuck you, now."

Ian watched as her eyes went wide and then flashed with a primal arousal that only a Dom could truly appreciate. He heard his own groan of satisfaction as she let herself down over his cock, impaling herself in one slow, torturous slide. She was so tight from the plug that Jace had pushed into her nether hole that he was fighting for his own control the instant he felt her muscles start to flutter around him. He looked up and saw her eyes were closed. "Open your eyes, pet. I want your gaze locked on mine. If you close your eyes again, I'll consider it an attempt to close me out—like not taking my calls—and you'll get added swats tomorrow night for it." Honestly, his words were more for his own benefit than hers. He was desperately trying to maintain his control, and he was grasping wildly at straws for any distraction.

He was pleased to see her comply immediately, and he smiled his approval. "Such a good girl. You are so very beautiful, love. I can't begin to tell you how much you are pleasing us both." He flexed his pelvic muscles, causing his cock to shift inside her, and he watched the pulse point at the base of her neck as her heart kicked up and her breathing became even shallower. "Now, lie down against my chest. That's exactly right. Now relax your muscles and let Master Jace remove the plug so he can replace it with something that is going to give you a lot more pleasure."

The lounger they were using had been designed by Ian, and he considered it one of his best ideas ever. It was beautifully crafted out of mahogany with thick padding and a tufted leather top. It was the perfect height to allow his sweet sub to fuck herself with his cock just by flexing her knees as she straddled his body. And it was narrow enough that she wouldn't tire out quickly and Ian had only to move his legs to the side to spread hers further apart and make room for Jace to position himself behind her and slip into her ass.

When Callie pressed her breasts against his chest, she groaned at the sensation, and he knew that the hair on his chest would feel particularly abrasive against her ultrasensitive nipples. He could hardly wait until tomorrow night—seeing her in nipple clamps and chains was going to be a wet dream come true. Tomorrow was going to be a test of sorts for her. If she weathered the storm they had planned for her, he would never let her go.

Ian wrapped his left arm tightly around her, hell, she was so tiny his arm easily encircled her entire back. He used his right hand to run small circles at the small of her back. That was a sensitive spot for many women, but he'd noticed it was a particularly responsive area for Callie. Almost immediately she was lifting into his touch. He pressed down and warned, "Stay still, pet. Let Master Jace work his magic on your sweet little ass."

* * * *

All of Callie's best intentions to keep her heart out of Ian's reach had clearly been nuked, there just wasn't any other possible explanation. *Well, there was always the possibility that I've finally gone completely over the edge of sanity, but really like the nuked idea better.* She'd been glad when Ian had pulled her against his chest because holding his gaze had just been too intense. His eyes alone could push her over the ledge into the free fall of orgasm. At least now that she wasn't face-to-face with him she could close her eyes and bask in his and Jace's combined touches. Ian's hand moving in small circles on her lower back felt deliciously possessive. That spot had always been particularly sensitive for her. Feeling Ian's hand pressing against her as they'd walked in to Club Isola the other night had almost made her knees go out from under her.

She moaned as Jace fucked her ass with the plug before removing it. She felt the cool gel and then the searing heat of his cockhead as he began pressing into her. *Oh my God in heaven, he's so huge! How will he ever fit? And Ian is already taking up a lot of my real estate.* "Oh God, you are both so huge. And I really don't think you are both going to fit inside me. But if I die from this, I'm going to go as one very happy camper, I just thought you should know."

She screamed as Jace slammed the rest of the way in her. He had gotten part way in and then given her the rest of his length in one sudden thrust. She felt herself starting to climax and knew she didn't have their permission to let go yet, so she was desperately trying to think of anything to distract her. She remembered having to learn the Gettysburg Address in American Government, so she started reciting that in her head. But as soon as she got to the part about all men being created equal she got sidetracked because it was so obviously not true. Really, it was completely false if you asked her. After all, these men were endowed with more than the average person's inalienable rights…oh wait, that was the US Constitution…no, that was from the Declaration of Independence. Yeah, that's right…Damn, she just realized she'd said all of that out loud because she heard the soft chuckles from both men.

Ian pushed her up enough to look in to her eyes. "Pet, I have to tell you that was one amazing little journey your mind took. Were you by chance trying to distract yourself so that you wouldn't come without permission?" She knew he wasn't angry because his eyes had laugh lines surrounding them, but she wasn't going to be snarky and risk flipping his "pissy-switch" either.

She held his gaze even though she knew her face was bright red with embarrassment. She finally managed to answer, "Yes. That is exactly what I was trying to do. I didn't want to let you down, and that was the only thing I could think of. But I sure wish I hadn't said all that out loud. Geez, this is so embarrassing. But on the plus side, I was able to pull back....oh God." Just as she'd been about to finish her sentence, they had started moving in and out of her openings so that she had one of them deeply inside her at all times. As Ian pushed against her cervix, Jace would pull back so that the rim of the head of his cock teased the outer ring of muscles surrounding her back hole. And then in a carefully choreographed dance they reversed their movements in a pace far too slow for her liking. As she started trying to push them to go faster, Ian gave her a sharp slap to her ass cheek.

"Stop trying to take the reins, *Carlin*. That is known as 'topping from the bottom,' and it will always be dealt with quickly and harshly. That was your only warning. Now stay still and let us take our pleasure as we send you into orbit." And good to his word they started picking up the pace until she truly didn't know anything existed outside of the sensation of having the two of them pushing her body to new heights with each push and tilt of their cocks. She was so close she was worried she wouldn't be able to hold out any longer when she felt Ian shift his hips forward, and at the exact moment his cock hit the spongy spot at the front of her vagina, he shouted, "Come for us, my love!" and her entire world exploded. She felt as if she had been vaporized by the heat of the two men fucking her and that her entire body had broken up into bits of matter. There was no way she would ever recover, she was sure she was going to die from pure pleasure. She rode wave after wave of her release, and their shouts of completion and the feeling of their seed shooting in hot jetting shots deep inside her sent her over again. Just as she heard herself scream, everything went black and her mind shut down.

Chapter 20

Ian couldn't remember a time when he had awakened as refreshed as he felt this morning. The scene last night with Callie had been sensational. They had literally fucked her unconscious, and the primal part of him wanted to beat his chest à la Tarzan with pride at that fact. After they'd cleaned up and then carefully tended to Callie, he'd curled against her and slept like a baby. He'd only awakened midmorning because she'd been trying to slip from his arms to use the restroom.

He'd been locked away in his office for several hours catching up on e-mails and returning phone calls he'd missed while tending to his sweet sub last night. He was quickly realizing how much his entire life had centered on work these past few years. Hell, when a few hours off yielded this much of a backlog he'd obviously narrowed his life down to the point that he had little outside of his work. His friends and staff had been telling him as much for a while now, but it hadn't been until this morning that their words of caution had truly struck home.

As he had watched Callie leave his bed this morning gloriously naked, her hair tousled into a mass of riotous blonde curls giving her a well-earned *just fucked* appearance, something inside his soul had recognized just how right it felt. He knew in that instant that letting her go wasn't ever going to be an option, but could he give up his chosen lifestyle if she didn't get through tonight's "test"? He could only hope he didn't have to find out.

* * * *

Ian had arranged for Callie to spend the day with Dee Tate, he knew the two women had seemed to hit it off when they'd met at the club last weekend. He also knew that because of Dee's commitment to her submissive lifestyle, she would be a great source of information and would openly answer any of Callie's questions. Mike and Dee would be working at Club Isola tonight so they wouldn't be attending the party. He'd originally planned on pulling them off their duties as he had the others, but had later decided he didn't want to risk Callie feeling embarrassed in front of her new friend by what she was going to experience tonight. For experienced subs it was usually a shared point of bonding, but he wasn't sure Callie would understand that at this point, so he'd decided there wouldn't be any other submissives present.

An hour later he heard her enter the back sliding doors, and he smiled when she knocked softly on the frame of his open office door. "Come in, pet. Come here and tell me about your afternoon adventures." She didn't hesitate to walk to him as he held his hand out to her. She smelled like flowers and sunshine as he pulled her onto his lap.

"Dee and I had such fun. She showed me where you are thinking of building a resort, and we talked about all the possibilities for gardens and amenities. She's an interior decorator, did you know that? Oh...of course you did. Anyway, she has wonderful tastes, and her ideas for your project are top notch. You really should consider hiring her when the time comes." Her words had bubbled out of her with a childlike enthusiasm that made him laugh. "Oh...I'm sorry, that was pretty pushy of me, wasn't it? I didn't mean it disrespectfully. It's just that she is so talented, and I kind of got caught up in the whole thing."

His heart wretched at her soft words of apology. *Fuck, didn't anybody every give this poor girl any encouragement at all?* "Oh, *Carlin*, I wasn't laughing at you in a bad way. I was just happy that you had a good time and that you are interested in the project because I'd like to talk with you about that next week." Leaning down, he kissed her on the end of her nose. "Let's get through this evening and then work on what's next, how's that sound? This is a good opportunity for you to understand the joys of not needing to worry about anything but pleasing your Master, because what would please me right now is for you to keep that enthusiasm alive and well because I plan to tap it soon enough."

Moving her so that she was standing next to him, he gave her what he knew was a devilish look. "But right now, you, my lovely pet, are wearing entirely too many clothes. Your master likes to look at you and wants unrestricted access, remember?" Her reaction was instant and textbook perfect—eyes dilated, pulse and respiration rates increased. "Strip, pet." As she quickly shed her clothing, he stood in front of her, taking each article after she'd folded it and laying it on the corner of his desk.

"Perfect. I see you got a bit of sun today. We'll have to work on evening out those tan lines in a few days. Kneel, pet." As she lowered herself gracefully in front of him, he stepped closer and stood with his feet braced shoulder width apart with his hands resting on his hips. "Your Master is in need of some relief, pet. Pleasure me. Suck me hard and fast, and I want you to drink every drop down. You have five minutes to break my control, if you fail I'll clamp your clit so that you can't come and then fuck you until I can't hold out any longer." He loved how her eyes widened at the challenge, and if he was honest, he figured her devil-blessed mouth would bring him to completion in no time at all. He looked at his watch and then at her. "What are you waiting for? Best get busy, pet."

It was difficult to suppress his smile as she scrambled to get his jeans unfastened and lowered, but it was impossible to hold back the groan of relief when his raging hard-on was finally freed from its tight confines. Since he hadn't forbidden her from using her hands, he didn't point out that he hadn't given her permission to use them while pleasuring him either. This wasn't a "set up to fail" situation, it was more about getting her into the right state of mind for tonight's activities.

She used the tip of her hot tongue to delve into his slit, scooping out the pre-cum that had gathered there. Licking up and back down his length and then swallowing him down her throat had been a small glimpse of heaven, but when she moaned around him, he knew he wasn't going to last. He began thrusting in her cajoling mouth, she had coaxed his control right out from under him, and now his only thought was to chase the pleasure that he knew awaited him as he watched her taking every one of his thick inches. His hands wrapped around her lovely face, and his fingers tangled in her hair, and when she looked up at him, her eyes full of pleasure, he threw his head back and shouted his completion. "Oh fuck, Callie! Your mouth is going to be the death of me, my love." As he tried to slow his breathing, he used his thumb to catch a small drop of his semen at the corner of her mouth. Spreading it over her lower lip, his breath caught in his chest when her pink tongue darted out as if it were trying to retrieve a treasure before it was snatched away. "You are so very beautiful. And you have pleased me very much."

He pulled his pants up and fastened them, glancing up at the smirking cowboy leaning his shoulder against the door frame grinning like a loon. He helped her stand, but kept her facing him while he spoke. "I'm going to remind you that you are stunning and I love seeing every sweet inch of you. And if it pleases me for others to see you, remember it would be an insult to me for you to feel self-conscious. Do you understand, pet?"

God, he loved watching arousal flash through her eyes as he crashed through a new barrier. "Y–yes, Master, I understand. You don't want me to feel embarrassed by the man standing in the doorway behind me, is that right?" To her credit, her lips might have twitched, but she managed to contain the smile, the little imp. Gage's snort of laughter let Ian know he'd heard her soft words.

"Minx, get your clothes and head on upstairs. Take a nice long bath and then put on what has been laid out for you—nothing more and nothing less. You don't need to be back down here for a while, so take your time. Leave your hair down, I want to be able to wrap my hands in it when it pleases me to do so." Swatting lightly on the ass, he turned her to face Gage. "Callie, I'd like you to meet Gage Hughes. Gage will be attending tonight's get-together so you'll be getting to know him much better. Like I mentioned last night, each of our guests tonight has a very specific specialty, can you guess what Gage's is, *Carlin?*"

He watched as her face tinged a sweet pink that reminded him of cotton candy before she looked back at him. "No, Master, I'm sorry, I have no idea. But I know he is a former member of the military, probably special forces and very recently, too. I also know he hails from the south, likely Texas, and that he has spent a lot of time on the back of a horse."

Holy fuck! What was that about? How the hell did she know all that from looking at the man for thirty seconds? Ian was completely stunned, and from the look on Gage's face, he was equally as surprised. "Well, I'm impressed Callie, very impressed. Would you please share with us exactly how you know these things? Which are dead-on, I might add."

She smiled and flicked her gaze to Gage before returning it to him. "Well, I'm pretty good with body language, Sir. And well, I'm a bit of an empath. I'm not as good as Mitch Grayson, but I'm not completely without skills either. But to be fair, the horse part was easy, see the stirrup marks on the sides of his boots? And the heels are scuffed from the spurs he uses." Her eyes were absolutely dancing with joy. She was clearly enjoying the fact that she'd blindsided him by knowing about Mitch Grayson. Hell, he couldn't wait to talk to Mitch himself. She leaned forward and kissed him on the cheek. "And by the way, Sir. Thank you for your concern…having me talk with Mr. Grayson was very sweet and helpful as well."

He pulled her into his embrace and buried his face against her soft tresses. "Woman, you are going to pay for this, you know that, right?" He knew she would hear the laughter in his voice and know he wasn't really angry. "Now, upstairs with you, impertinent sub."

She smiled and picked up her clothes before making her way to the door. Gage stepped aside and nodded to her. "Nice to meet you, Callie, damned impressive. You would have been a valuable member of our team." He let his eyes sweep slowly down and then back up in a warm visual caress. "I'm looking forward to tonight's party even more now." He was rewarded by a sweet smile and blush before she simply nodded and scooted by him.

After they were sure she was safely out of hearing range, he looked over at Ian and laughed out loud. "Holy fucking hell, I didn't think I'd ever live long enough to see you speechless, boss man. That is one impressive woman you have there. You might want to tone things down a bit this evening. Damn, I'd hate to see you screw this up. Then again, maybe I'd be able to pick up the pieces of her broken heart. Yeah, let's leave everything just the way it's been set up."

Ian shook his head and laughed. "Fuck you, Hughes. And for the record, I can't remember the last time I was so completely caught off guard. She is amazing, and I don't have any intention of losing her. And I think that with her newly revealed skills, I may need to tone things down a bit because I'm fairly certain she would pick up on my concerns. And the last thing I want to do is risk losing her."

Chapter 21

Callie had stayed in the upstairs spa bath so long she wasn't sure her legs were going to hold her up when she'd finally decided to surface. She was buffed, polished, and she'd brushed her hair until it lay in silky waves all the way to the top of her ass. She loved how it felt moving over her sensitized skin. She'd opted for minimal makeup, reasoning that she would be shedding tears and there was nothing attractive about smeared mascara. She'd peeked into the bedroom earlier and was amazed to see the dress Ian had placed over the end of the bed. It was a deep-purple silk with random threads of various shades of gold. It was perfect for her, it would highlight her eyes and her hair, and the style would accentuate her petite frame. *Gotta give the guy credit, he's got a wicked fashion sense. Shit, he's really pretty wicked all the way around.* She snickered at her own joke only to hear Ian's voice from the corner. "Care to share that thought, pet?" *Holy pickle fudge, how did I miss him sitting over there?*

"Well, not really, but I'm betting you're going to insist, so I probably should just fess up, huh?" She finally realized she was sliding the soft fabric of the dress between her fingers, thinking about how it was going to feel hugging her curves. When he didn't answer, but just continued to watch her intently, she continued. "I was just thinking that you have a…um, well, a wicked fashion sense…and that sort of led to me thinking that there are other parts of you that are deliciously wicked also…and…" She didn't finish, she could already see the smile on his face, and she felt her blush all the way to her toes.

"You really are a joy. Come here, pet. I want to talk to you for a bit before we go downstairs." As she approached him, she noticed he'd already showered and shaved and dressed in all black, and he looked every bit the Dominant she knew he would be tonight. He seemed undecided about something, and for a few seconds she worried that he had already grown tired of the drama that seemed to have followed her to the island. But really, who could blame him? How on earth did she think she was worth all this trouble?

When she refocused, she was sitting on his lap, and he was studying her intently. "You are thinking too much, but I must admit, I love the fact that you think out loud. No, I have not grown tired of you, quite the opposite actually." Ian paused and took a couple of deep breaths. He couldn't remember a time he'd been so unsure as to what was the right approach with a submissive he was planning a scene with. But so far, he'd done a lot wrong with the one woman who actually mattered. And after talking with Gage, he'd decided it was time to fix that.

"Ordinarily when a Dom and his or her submissive are planning a scene there is a lot of negotiation involved, including hard limits, etc. I can tell by your expression you have at least some understanding of what I'm talking about. Anyway, because of the—shall we say *forced* nature of our relationship, we haven't done that, and I'm not sure that was in your best interests."

She was so unbelievably perfect for him, and he couldn't for the life of him imagine what he could have done that would have caused the Universe to deliver her, literally, to his door. She was going to get her scene tonight, but it was going to be something altogether different from what he'd originally envisioned. Never let it be said he wasn't a wise enough captain to know when to change course.

"Master?" Her sweet voice was full of concern, not for herself, but for him—it was written all over her face, and it touched him in a way he thought he'd never feel again.

"Callie, I know we have only been together a short time, but I think you will understand what I'm talking about when I say we seem to share a very unique connection." At her shy nod he went on. "We'll still be having guests tonight, but the focus of the evening is going to be more about showing you all the ways BDSM can bring you pleasure rather than trying to deliberately push you away, which is what I had been doing with people for a very long time—but that is a conversation for another day. And you'll be getting those pretty pink nipples clamped, but not just yet." Smiling at her confusion, he leaned forward and kissed her with a newfound purpose.

"Come on, my precious pet, let's get that dress on you and make our way downstairs. Oh, and you'll still be getting those last sixteen swats—don't think I've forgiven those."

* * * *

Dinner had been wonderful, and Callie hadn't even minded the fact that she was the only woman at the table. What had been distracting was the fact that she'd had on a beautiful dress as they'd entered the dining room but nothing else. She had thought she would die of embarrassment when she realized the dress only looked opaque because it was lying on the bed. When Ian had lifted it over her head she had easily been able to see everything in the room, and it didn't take a rocket scientist to know if she could see *out* of the dress every Dom at the party was going to be able to see *in* as well. The minute she had stepped into the room, her suspicions had been confirmed by the smiles and comments of approval she'd received as she'd been introduced to their guests.

Ian had made sure she pulled the dress up in the back when she sat on the cold chair and then the cad had actually laughed at her startled gasp. Damn wood was cold on her bare pussy, no other way to say it. And even though they had enjoyed a relaxed dinner, the sexual tension was starting to build. It felt like static electricity in the air, making her skin prickle with anticipation. *Damn those sixteen swats, I hate having those hanging over my head...well, ass. When will I ever learn?*

Jace was seated at her left, and he burst out laughing. "Probably never, sweetness. Hell, you can't keep from thinking aloud, how the hell are you ever going to be able to concentrate enough to behave? And personally, I am sort of hoping you don't ever get it completely right." He winked at her and then said, "Ian, I believe you may have let this little goose stew about as long as you dare. Let's get this show on the road."

A part of Callie had been relieved at Ian's agreement, but a quick glance around the table had sent her into immediate *fight or flight* mode. She was shocked when the man who had been introduced to her as Kalen Black was the one to step up and speak to her. His hands cupped her shoulders, and he looked so deeply into her eyes, she had the feeling he was seeing clear to her soul. "Don't worry, angel. You are going to do fine. Just remember, you have a safe word, and when you have the chance to jump off in to sub-space—take it." He'd given her a quick hug and then turned her to Ian.

As she and Ian had followed the others down the hall, he had leaned over and whispered in her ear, "Pet, that may well be the most I have heard Kalen say at one time in all three years I've known him." He chuckled then added, "I'd say you must have made a pretty big impression on our resident student of the ancient mystics."

From the front of the group, Callie heard Kalen's soft voice. "The uninformed mock what they don't understand, boss." All the men laughed, but Callie was still thinking about what he'd said about taking the chance to jump off into sub-space. She'd read about the endorphin-induced euphoria, and now she wondered if that was what had caused her fuzzy feeling at Club Isola during the flogging. And holy hell on a hippo, she was fairly certain Kalen could get woman to do whatever he wanted using nothing more than his voice. She was certain the angels themselves sounded just like Kalen. He reminded her of a panther. He was just under six feet tall and with a sleek body build and jet-black hair highlighting his electric blue eyes. He moved with a catlike grace, and it seemed like he just kind left one spot and appeared in another.

Logan Douglas had been one of the men watching them on the terrace last night. When they had told her that he was an explosives expert he'd given her a wicked grin. "It's true, sugar. I love to watch things explode, including sweet little subs." His southern-boy charm made her smile. He might be a rogue, but she couldn't help but think he'd be a real gentleman to his woman…well, maybe outside of the club and their bedroom.

The cowboy Ian had introduced her to earlier in his office was also in attendance. Gage Hughes was a true Texas charmer. His honey-colored hair and tanned skin topped off a muscular body. She noticed his accent was thicker when he was "bein' charmin'," and that appeared to be most of the time. But there was a hardness about him that hadn't escaped her attention either. The man was certainly no pushover, that was for sure.

Jace had joined them as well, and she hadn't missed the fact he had flanked her other side in a move that looked almost protective in a big-brother, *but not*, sort of way. She already knew what perfection his clothing hid. His skin color was a wonderful honey brown, a testament to his mother's Native American heritage. He'd told her about his parents' ranching operation in Texas, and she'd heard the homesickness in his voice. When she had mentioned it, he'd assured her he would be heading home for a visit sometime after he took a little "swing through" southern Florida. Callie knew exactly why Jace was going to Miami. He was going to confront Chrissy about all the money she'd taken under false pretenses. Shaking off thoughts of her sister, Callie brought her mind purposefully back to the moment. She knew she'd need to keep her wits about her if she was going to get through the next few hours. It wasn't that she was afraid of the pain she was facing, it would be better described as worried she would let Ian down.

During dinner they had talked about all the crazy times they'd shared while building the club and getting members vetted. Their security clearance process alone rivaled most government positions, and they'd laughed about the reactions of various military officers, many with high-security clearance levels, who had not been cleared for Club Isola. They'd made it clear that their background checks were more current, and they'd teased Ian that he should offer to show the Joint Chiefs of Staff their reports—for a price, of course.

She'd been lost in thought and hadn't realized she and Ian were standing outside the open door of his personal playroom. Jace's huge frame completely filled the doorway, blocking her view, and obviously the others had already entered. Ian was watching her...again. "Welcome back, pet. Your capacity for mental road trips is astonishing sometimes. Someday I going to demand a detailed replay, but tonight I'm more interested in getting to other things." He smiled down at her, easing some of the tension she suddenly felt racing through her system. "There are rules that are strictly enforced as soon as you cross the threshold of this room, love. These rules are nonnegotiable, so best you listen closely." He waited for her nod before continuing.

"You may never enter this room unless you are naked, you will always strip in this hallway and leave your clothing neatly folded on this table." He pointed to a narrow table holding a small lamp near the door. "I can assure you, when you and I are home alone, you will always be naked." His grin was infectious, and she felt herself smile in return despite the elephants on roller skates doing pirouettes in her stomach. "And the moment you walk through that door, you will address each of the Dominants in the room with respect and by their proper titles. You will not speak unless you are asked a direct question, and you will follow each order immediately—hesitation will be punished—immediately and harshly. Do you have any questions, pet?" He had wrapped his hands loosely around her neck and was gently massaging the tense muscles at the base of her skull. She hadn't even realized how tense she'd become until he pressed the tips of his fingers into the taut muscles and whispered, "Relax, love, you will do fine." She felt her face heat and tears fill her eyes under his scrutiny. "Tell me what you are afraid of, Callie."

She was shocked at his use of her given name because he used it so rarely. And she was sure he'd done it deliberately to get her full attention. "I'm...well, I'm afraid of disappointing you, Master." She saw his eyes widen slightly, and then his expression softened.

"Your answer tells me more than you know, love. You will not disappoint me, I assure you. Let's go." And then he stepped back and she watched as his entire demeanor changed before her very eyes. He widened his stance and crossed his arms over his broad chest and said, "Strip, pet."

Chapter 22

Stepping over the threshold of Ian's playroom was akin to stepping back in time and place. She sucked in a breath and knew her mouth was gapping open as she slowly took in her surroundings. The entire room looked like something right out of a Middle Ages torture chamber. The walls were rough-cut rock, and the dim light emitted from the wall sconces cast eerie shadows that danced over the gray walls and slab floors. She recognized most of the equipment she could see from her reading and her visit to Club Isola. She wasn't sure where the other men had gone, and for some reason that kicked up her anxiety. Ian moved in front of her and tilted her chin up with one finger. "Welcome to my playroom, pet. Are you nervous?"

"Yes, sir." Callie had tried to steady her voice, but knew it hadn't worked.

"Do you trust me, Callie? Do you trust me to surround you with people you can trust to your last breath?" Ian's voice was warm and seductive, but there was a thread of steel that she didn't miss. She knew she did trust him, even though she didn't completely understand why, it was still true. She trusted Jace, too, and she knew the other men were here because they were trusted friends of both men. She nodded her head, but he said, "No, love, you have to say the words. We must always have very clear communication."

"I do trust you, even when I don't understand why, I know it's true." She kept her gaze on his, but felt someone step up behind her. At his first touch she knew it was Jace, and his hands stroked her arms from shoulder to wrist, and he then encircled her wrists, holding her as sure as if he'd handcuffed her.

"Sweetness, your trust is a gift. I promise you it's a gift your Master and every other man in this room with you tonight will treasure and protect forever." She saw the approval in Ian's eyes at his friend's words, and she relaxed a bit.

"They are ready for us, pet. Let's go—punishment first, then pleasure." Ian had switched back into the Dom she'd seen on several occasions, but this time she didn't feel so unsettled by the switch. She followed him over to what she knew was a spanking bench. She felt the shudder that worked its way down her spine, but she didn't step away. She let him guide her so that she knelt on to the padded squares on each end of the bench and then to lean over the padded top. While Ian secured wide leather cuffs around her wrists and then clipped them into place, she felt Jace strapping her legs down also. He'd placed one band around her leg just above her knee and another over at her ankle. It went through her mind that this seemed to be a bit of overkill since she would have been stable kneeling and leaning over the bench, when suddenly she heard a small motor engage and she felt herself being rotated forward. *Well, that explains all the straps. Cracker Jacks, I'm practically standing on my head...well, in a super kinky way. And let's just put my who-ha right up at the top all spread out for everyone to see. Yikes!*

She appreciated that Ian had kept a hand on her at all times, and if she strained her neck she could see him standing beside her. He leaned down and spoke close to her ear. "Stop stretching your neck, pet. You are going to hurt yourself. Are you in pain? Do you want to use your safe word?"

"No, I—well, I just wanted to see you...to know you were close. I'm sorry." She felt tears fill her eyes, she was disappointed in herself because she hadn't meant to do anything wrong.

Ian leaned over and kissed her temple. "No need to apologize. Actually I'm pleased that you are looking to me as an anchor. That shows trust, pet, thank you. But now, I want you to trust that I am not leaving this room. A Dom never leaves his sub tied, it's dangerous on many levels. But I want you to concentrate on what you are feeling, not seeing, so I'm going to put this over those beautiful violet eyes of yours." Callie jumped as the cool silk slid over her eyes and everything went black. She felt her heart speed up and knew they were ready to begin.

She could tell by his voice Ian had stood up, but he was still close. His voice was louder and authoritative. "You have sixteen swats coming. You'll get four from each man present. They will each be using their own personal favorite implement. As you know, I prefer to use my hand on your sweet ass. This will be more intense, so I will be monitoring your responses. What is your safe word, pet?"

"Red, Sir."

"Good enough. We'll begin." She felt the air shift around her and was just starting to panic when she felt a hand touch her lower back and then trail over her ass cheeks in a firm caress.

She knew the minute he spoke it was Gage. His Texas twang soothing to her ears. "Well, darlin', I'm not gonna draw this out because I promise you we are all anxious to get this over and done so we can enjoy the rest of our time together. I'm going to be using a wide paddle. It will bring the blood toward the surface and help you make it through what's to come. My spanks will come fast and hard, and I will not ask you to count them, because I do believe this ole country boy can count to four without any help." She barely had time to process his words before she heard a loud whoosh just before a loud smack and then fire lit up her ass. She screamed as much in surprise as pain. He didn't give her any time between the blows, he hadn't been kidding about fast and hard. When it was over she'd caught her breath and she heard him whisper, "Well done, darlin'," as he stepped away.

She was taking deep breaths trying to calm herself down when she felt the air shift again. Then another southern accent, but this one much softer—aw, the southern charmer, Logan. "Oh, sugar, your ass is a lovely deep pink. Master Gage did a fine job of warming you up."

Warming me up? Are you fucking kidding me? If that was a warm up I think I need to reevaluate my plan to stick around for the pleasure part of this little Dommie Dark Show. She felt him lean down and his words were spoken directly in her ear, "Might want to take care to not speak those thoughts aloud again, sugar." She gasped in surprise and firmly clamped her lips together. She'd heard the laughter in his voice and swore she'd heard a snort of laughter from off to the side, but she was determined to not screw up again.

When Logan moved back behind her again she felt something cool and soft moving over her hot ass cheeks. "Now, my Dom brothers each have very specific ideas about punishment techniques. But I think a Dom needs to be flexible and make sure what he uses is just right for the sub he's working with, so I'm going to be using something that can be used for pleasure or it can give a nice bite also. I'm also going to spread my strikes out so that you don't get too much in one spot." Just then she felt what felt like a dozen tiny sparks of pain. The blows were fast and didn't really hurt that much at first but by the time he'd finished the warm feeling had turned to red-hot flames. She was fairly certain you'd be able to smell her skin burning if you just tried.

She knew she was crying but didn't care because she had earned the pain, and it felt like it was working to break loose something dark inside of her. Just as she was starting to get her breathing back under control, she heard Kalen's voice and immediately felt like she'd been thrown a lifeline. "Angel, you are doing very well. You are making your Master very proud. He is a very fortunate man. The Universe sent him a very special gift in that little rowboat."

She heard murmurs of agreement from the side, but it was Ian's voice that stood out. "Yes, it did. A gift I plan to take very good care of, I assure you." And just that quickly, all the pain suddenly faded to the back of her mind. His declaration broke through the last barrier she'd erected, and she felt herself beginning to understand the power of submission. She felt more complete than she had in years.

"Aww, sweet angel. I can see by your body's response that your Master's words have gone straight to your heart, just as they were supposed to. I'm going to lay four stripes across your ass with a cane. The pain will be intense, but I want you to breathe through it, let it wash over you as you would the warm waves of the ocean on a hot summer day." She had been so entranced with his words she was totally unprepared for his first strike with the cane.

She felt the first two but then something in her mind broke, and she felt like she was floating outside her own body. It was as if she'd stepped through Alice's looking glass and everything was the opposite of what it should be, because the pain was nothing but pure, undiluted pleasure. She felt another pair of hands touching her and thought maybe she'd been tilted back up. Then she heard words that she didn't fully understand before she heard a sharp crack split the air. Following each loud crack there was icy, heated pleasure drawn in sharp lines diagonally down her ass. Two one direction and then two going the other way, and then she heard her Master tell her to come, and her entire world exploded into color. Someone was screaming, and she wondered if that woman was enjoying the same light show she was seeing.

Chapter 23

Watching Callie take the last half of her punishment with grace and dignity had been a life-changing experience for Ian. He knew that Gage hadn't hit her overly hard with the paddle, the pain she had felt was likely as much from surprise as real discomfort. And he'd had to work hard not to laugh out loud at her comments when Logan had referred to Gage's strokes as a warm-up. But as he'd watched her under Kalen's cane, he'd nearly stopped the scene. Thank God she'd gone immediately in to sub-space because her pain-filled scream had nearly shredded his heart.

As Jace had used the single-tail to lay four narrow strips of fire that Ian was sure she hadn't even registered, Kalen had stepped up alongside him. "Ian, I know this was hard for you. But she needed to prove to you that she could do it or she would never have felt worthy. She really is quite exquisite, and I meant what I told her. She is a wonderful gift. Let her into your heart—let her heal whatever it is that haunts you." Jace was the only one of his staff who knew any of the details of his past, but that didn't mean his other friends didn't know he was less than whole. He'd been very grateful for Kalen's words because he'd been questioning his decision to finish the scene, and now he was able to see that it had been necessary for both of them.

Ian stepped up as the others released Callie from the bench. They had rubbed her limbs, making sure the stiffness would be minimal, and then Ian stepped up with the benzo-aloe gel Mitch had invented. The stuff was perfect for sub aftercare because it had a topical anesthetic and also soothed the burn in deeper tissues. Considering Callie's inability to use most painkillers safely, he had decided this was the best option. They hadn't laid her on the bed to treat her because they'd wanted to make sure she was fully cognizant before beginning the part they'd all been looking forward to.

Ian stepped in front of Callie and smoothed the sweat-dampened curls from her tear-stained face. "You did so well, love. I am honored and humbled by your trust. And now I am looking forward to playing with you in a whole new—and much more pleasurable—way. Come on, love." Stopping next to the table they'd be using, he saw the concern in her expression despite not being able to see her eyes. "We've chosen this table because we'll all have easy access to you, it raises and lowers easily, and it is spectacularly comfortable—just don't fall asleep on us, pet." He smiled at her relieved expression. He could tell she had wanted to speak, but had caught herself before the words had made their way out. "Since this is a reward, I'm going to let you speak unless you are specifically told not to—but, I want you to remember to keep your words respectful. We will all enjoy hearing your pleasure, *Carlin*."

Ian leaned forward and kissed her on the very tip of her nose. "Enjoy, baby—you have earned this treat." He slowly turned her so that she faced Kalen. "Kalen will be starting things off, I'll let him explain." He stepped back and couldn't help the small bit of satisfaction he got from seeing her quick glance to confirm he was still close. Her shy smile warmed his heart. She *belonged* to him, and he was pleased that her heart seemed to be catching up with her soul.

He never tired of hearing Kalen explain the link between massage and the release of sexual energy so that it could freely flow to all parts of the body. Watching as Kalen explained the joys of Tantric massage, it was easy to see excitement and interest in her body language. Her entire body was flushing, and he smiled as she enthusiastically nodded her assent. Ian had heard more than one sub say that Kalen's voice alone was enough to get them off, and judging by Callie's rapt attention, he was starting to think it might be true.

He stepped up to listen and watch after Kalen had gotten his beautiful sub settled on the bench. The hole in bottom for her lovely face allowed her to stay flat and kept her spine straight. Kalen explained all the intricacies of spinal alignment as he began with soft touches to awaken nerve endings. It was interesting to listen as his friend wove a web of seduction tighter around Callie until there was nowhere to go and her only escape was to surrender to the desire.

As he worked her sore shoulders and back muscles, Ian could hear her soft sighs. But as Kalen's hands moved further down, the sighs became soft moans of pleasure. Kalen leaned over and said, "Open your legs for me, angel. I want to feel my fingers sliding through your beautiful pussy. The ancients likened it to a rose that opens when the woman is aroused."

Ian knew the instant Kalen had put his fingers inside because he heard her softly whispered, "Yes, oh God, yes, it feels so good." His cock was so hard he was sure he was going to have a permanent zipper imprint. Kalen looked up and nodded once and then Ian saw him rotate his wrist slightly and knew his friend was pressing on the soft, spongy spot that would send Callie flying in no time.

"Does that feel good, angel-girl? Hold your release for me. Don't come yet, hold off for me. It'll be so much sweeter." Ian could hear the sweet slurping sounds of Callie's pussy milking Kalen's fingers and saw her stiffen just as Kalen whispered, "Come for me, angel." Ian wished he could see her face, she was always so beautiful when she was lost in the throes of release.

Kalen had assured him that she would be totally energized after the orgasm he would give her, and Ian was pleased to see Callie seemed hyperaware as he helped her sit up. Smoothing the backs of his fingers down her soft cheeks, he couldn't help but smile at the look of anticipation on her face. "It sounded like you enjoyed Master Kalen's massage, pet. Tell me."

"Oh, Master, it was amazing. I feel like I have so much more energy now. I really think you guys shouldn't tease him about studying those ancient mystics. Holy crapping crickets it is amazing, and you should really try it sometime, seriously." He finally placed his fingers over her lips, stilling her. Hell, he was worried she wasn't ever going to come up for air. How the hell could anyone talk so long without stopping to breathe anyway?

"Pet, if it was a couple's massage class, perhaps I'd join you, but Master Kalen is not going to be giving me a massage—*ever*." He heard the other men's laughter from the back of the room. "Now, Masters Logan and Gage will be working together, so lie back down and enjoy. When they are finished, Master Jace and I will be taking you back to the master suite. We have something special planned for you." He knew she was surprised when he turned her around and Logan and Gage were standing right behind her. *Damn special ops guys move like fucking cats, used to spook the shit out of me, too, Callie. God, she is amazing. She's smart, sweet, and submissive to the bone. And she's MINE!*

* * * *

Callie had been surprised when Ian turned her, and she came face-to-face with Logan. "Oh, sugar, we are going to make you feel so good. Let's get you up on to this nice comfy table. There you go. Now, lie back. Master Kalen's treatment was focused on your back, and we're going to make sure this beautiful front receives equal attention." Callie smiled up at him and wondered how she was ever going to survive being the focus of these two Doms' southern charms. As she lay back she thought about the fact that she was stark naked in a room with five Dominant Alpha men and she wasn't even frightened. Heck, she'd been afraid of being in a room alone with a man for years. But there wasn't any fear at all with these men.

Suddenly she noticed Gage standing over her looking at her intently. He smiled and glanced up at Ian. "You're right, boss, she does check out now and again. Hmm, let's see if we can't take care of your woman's distraction problem for a bit, shall we?" *Did he just call me Ian's woman? Oh boy.*

Logan stepped up on the other side of the table and held up a pair of strange things that looked like a circle within a circle with little set screws on each side. They were connected by a beautiful gold chain that looked like it had been braided using white, yellow, and rose gold. Running it through his fingers, Logan looked up at her and asked, "Pretty isn't it, sugar?" When she agreed with him, he held up the small circles and inquired about them as well. "Do you know what these are?"

"No, well, not really, but…well, maybe. I read a couple of Master's…oh, drat." She hadn't intended to mention raiding Ian's library, and now she'd busted herself right out.

She heard Ian's soft chuckle from the shadows to her left. "Pet, I knew you'd read the books in the library. You are welcome to read anything in there, I was pleased you were interested. Every room in the house except the master bath is wired for sight and sound as a safety measure. Also something you might want to remember should you decide to slide those beautiful fingers over your achy pussy during the night—again."

Stick a fork in me, I'm done. If it's possible to die of embarrassment, I'm a goner. "Yes, Master. I'm sorry, but I *missed* you."

Logan leaned down and whispered in her ear, "Nice save, sugar— very nice. You think quick, I'm impressed." He leaned back up and smiled down at her. "Well, these are nipple clamps. They are perfect for your first time, but as you may have guessed, my part of this evening's activities is to make sure these lovely breasts get some very special attention. I love women's breasts. They are the soft pillows of mankind. They nurture our children and soothe the sobs of an aching heart with a soft hug. And they're mighty fine for playing with, too." He leaned down and sucked on first one and then the other nipple until she was squirming beneath the onslaught of his mouth and tongue. He gripped the tender flesh with his teeth and teased the tips in to ever tighter points until they were so achy she wasn't sure she could take any more, and then he slipped the rings over her nipples and started turning the small screws until she gasped at the pressure. He paused, looked at her with an evil grin, and gave each another twist before he pronounced them to be perfect. "Those look lovely on you, they are a part of a set. Master Gage has the other pieces. They're our 'Welcome to the island' gift for you. And I'm sure your Master will enjoy them as well."

She was fighting to stay focused on his words. Was he insane? If so she hoped to Jesus it wasn't contagious, but the evidence didn't look very hopeful because every man in the room seemed to understand exactly what Logan was saying. Her nipples felt like they were being licked by fire. Oh shit, licking yes—but by the devil himself. *Gift? What the fuck? What happened to bubble bath and sweet-smelling soaps or maybe a nice bottle of wine—yeah, now there was a welcome to the island gift I would have appreciated.* When she heard soft chuckles she knew she'd done it again. "Oh shit, I mean, drat. I said that out loud, didn't I? Lord help me, when am I ever going to learn? I tell you all way too much that way, but it's just so much and it really hurts…a lot. And I don't know when my boobs got put online with my pu…um, well…some other parts. It's just too much sometimes and my overload switch must be connected to my mouth." *Just shoot me now.*

Gage moved into her field of vision and held a strip of black silk where she could see it. "I'm going to blindfold you, darlin', because that sharp little mind of yours wants to process everything at lightning speed and then those thoughts just can't help but tumble out of your mouth. And honest to God, it amuses the shit outta me, but it's distracting as hell, so we've got to get it under control before you earn yourself some more swats, and we have other things planned for you." He didn't waste any time shrouding her world in darkness. "Now, you'll be able to keep busy concentrating on what you are feeling, and maybe that will quiet your mind, darlin'." He was running his fingers down the side of her face and then just kept up the featherlight touch as he trailed down her neck. He moved around the nipple clamps, and she heard him saying how lovely she looked with her nipples all swollen and begging for attention and how he couldn't wait to give her the rest of her gift.

Somewhere in the back of her mind she wondered what else they could have for her, hell, didn't jewelry come in necklace and earring sets anymore? Geez, where did these guys shop anyway? Pervs Jewelers? Can't you just imagine the jingle for that store? Thankful she had managed to keep her thoughts quiet for once, she was starting to feel kind of floaty…was that even a word? But then she felt someone strapping down her legs to the table. They had placed straps just above her knees and at her ankles. She was relieved that at least this once her legs weren't spread from here to eternity. Just as she was planning her little happy dance of regained dignity, she felt a strange rumbling coming from under her ass. *Shit, is that a motor? Oh cracker jacks, this can't be good.* Her legs glided apart and bent up at the knees while her head seemed to be tilting down further.

Just as she was going to open her mouth to speak, warm fingers pressed against her lips. "Think first, sugar—are you getting ready to say your safe word?"

"Un, no, Master Logan, I was just—" She was cut off when he pressed his fingers to her lips again.

"Then you don't have permission to speak. If I were you, I'd exercise your constitutional right to remain silent that so many subs forget about." She heard the smile in his voice and was grateful that he'd helped her avoid making another mistake. She nodded her head and pressed her lips together. "Good girl. Now, about those clamps."

As soon as he'd spoken the words she'd felt a tug on the chain between her breasts, and her nipples were once again set aflame. "Ahhh…Oh God…Oh God…"

"Now that is the sort of thing we enjoy hearing, sugar." Logan's voice was like auditory sin. Geez, his voice was nearly as hot as Kalen's.

Callie felt the air around her stir and assumed he'd moved to her other side. But before she could figure it out, she felt fingers lightly stroking her outer labia. They didn't get any closer or the strokes didn't seem to be intensifying and still she felt her pussy sending juices to coat the fingers of her tormentor. She heard herself moan and tried to lift her pelvis into the touch, but all she accomplished was getting a stinging swat directly over her pussy. "Ahhhh…"

"Darlin', this is gonna work on our timetable, not yours, so you just lie back and enjoy and no more toppin' from the bottom. Because, babe, I gotta tell ya—this isn't Master Logan's or my first rodeo, and we will recognize that for what it is and deal with it in ways that you don't want to know about." What happened to her sweet Texas charmer? *Damn, isn't that just how it works, I think I have them pegged and then they go all Big Bad Dom on me.* "Oh, I can tell by your body language you are thinking again, little subbie, well, I'm gonna light you up, darlin', and let's see how much free time you have for a mental road trip then, shall we?"

The thread of challenge in his voice wasn't lost on her, and just as she tried to figure out what he might be planning he plunged his fingers in so deep she was sure he'd brushed her cervix, which had only heightened the feeling. She felt her channel stretching and the small tremors that started to ripple around his fingers, and just as she was starting to really feel like she might be going to get some relief, he pulled his fingers out of her and tapped directly on top of her clit. Oh Lord, what had made her think she was going to have an easier time at these two southern charmers' hands? She tried to get her breathing under control, and as she started to feel oxygen was actually making its way into her brain again, she felt Gage begin what could only be described as an all-out oral assault. His kisses along the insides of her thighs were peppered with small nips of his teeth and then soothed with his tongue in a random pattern that had her constantly guessing where he'd move next. The only thing predictable about his movements was their complete unpredictability. It didn't matter that she'd already had multiple orgasms in the last twenty-four hours, her body was still chasing the next one with the same desperation as it had the first.

Logan leaned down and ran his tongue around the rim of her ear before biting down on the lobe. The pain morphed to pleasure and raced toward her clit after a short pit stop to torture her clamped nipples. "Felt that all the way to your sweet little clit, didn't you, sugar? You are one responsive little sub, that's for sure. Ian McGregor is a lucky bastard, and we've all told him exactly that, baby girl." She knew he was bringing her back to the moment again, and she found herself lost in his whispered words. "I'm going to enjoy watching you come apart under our touch, there is nothing more beautiful in the world than a woman as she hands over the power of her pleasure to a worthy man. And I promise you this—every man in this room is worthy of your submission. Be a brave girl now—jump—we'll be right here to catch you." With a last assault to her ear, he started a trail of blazing kisses down the side of her neck. When he reached her collarbones, he pressed his lips against the pulse point at the base of her neck, and she heard him say, "She's ready for your gift, Master Gage."

Immediately she felt Gage move his fingers all around her clit, and she groaned an unintelligible sound of appreciation at the tiny electrical pulses that felt like they were trying to travel from one part of her body to the other but weren't quite able to make the connection. She felt him pull the hood back and knew that her clit must be completely exposed to his view. "Beautiful, Callie. Your clit is all shiny and swollen, and it's just begging for my attention. Take a deep breath for me, darlin'. Good girl—now another. There you go, perfect."

Immediately she felt like he'd set her clit on fire. She screamed and thrashed her head back and forth. She heard a woman shouting, "No, no, it's too much…Oh Heavenly God save me." And she was grateful her mind caught up with her mouth before she finished the thought because she'd been sure she was going to die a horrible death at the hands of these sexual deviants.

Logan was back up at her ear, whispering, "Breathe through it, Callie. Listen to me, you can do this. It is going to be sweeter than you can even imagine if you will just ride it through for a few more seconds. Aha, I can tell by your reactions you are starting to feel it, aren't you? Tell me the truth, sugar. You've ridden the wave to the other side haven't you?"

"Oh God, Master Logan, it hurt so much…and I…I would have given up if you hadn't helped me…you helped me get here and it hurts so good. But I need…I…" She hadn't even gotten to finish because he put his fingers against her lips.

"Oh, sweet subbie, we know exactly what you need, and if you will just let us, we'll take you right to heaven's door." She could hear the strain in his voice and wondered why none of them had asked her to pleasure them. Maybe they didn't really think she was all that desirable, they were probably just doing this as a favor for Ian. Oh damn and wasn't that just about the most humiliating thing she'd ever experienced. Suddenly she was shaking all over, and she heard her own sobs a second before she felt another pair of hands alongside her face. And the blindfold was pushed aside, and all she could see was Ian's worried face.

"Pet, what's happened? Talk to me." She heard the desperation in Ian's voice, and she was suddenly mortified by her own insecurities and neediness.

"I'm sorry…so sorry. But I have to know…none of the men has asked me to…well, you know, give them any satisfaction, and well, do they think I'm not desirable or damaged or something? Because if they are only doing this as a favor to you, I swear I'll die of humiliation."

Ian smiled at her and leaned down to her ear. "Oh, my precious pet, I assure you each man in this room finds you very desirable. Hell, my little gift from God, I'm the envy of every man on this fucking island. All of us have had to leave the room at times because we were just too close to losing control. No, my sweet girl, no one fucks that lovely pussy but Jace or I. And this is a reward, remember? So you get to just sit back and enjoy. Now, are you all right to continue?" He'd smoothed the hair back from her face in loving sweeps of his fingers.

"Yes, Master. Thank you for your patience. I lo…um, I am lucky that you…well, I'm grateful. Thank you." She'd come so close to screwing everything up and further humiliating herself by letting him know how much she cared for him. She couldn't imagine how painful it was going to be to have to leave when he tired of her.

"Very good, pet. Now, play nice, sweet sub, because I have broken one of my own cardinal rules by interrupting another Dom's scene—something I'm sure I'll be hearing about for years to come."

Before he could pull away, she said, "Thank you…thank you for being my knight in shining armor…Master."

She saw his smile as he pulled the blindfold back over her eyes. And she heard his muttered "minx" before she knew he'd moved away simply because she felt the loss clear to her soul.

"Well, let's get something cleared up right now, shall we?" She felt her right hand being released and then her wrist rotated so that her palm was facing away from her body. And then suddenly her hand was pressed up against a very hard cock covered by leather that actually felt hot to the touch. "That is what you have done to every man in the room tonight, sugar. Make no mistake about how desirable you are. Remember, we are rewarding you, and we're big boys, we'll actually survive. Contrary to what every teenage boy in the world has told his date, we won't die from denying our release." He quickly secured her hand again, and before he'd even finished, Gage had started moving through her folds again with a firm touch that let her know that their little chat was over.

"I'm tired of the chatter, sweetie. Time for some real playtime, relax every muscle in your delectable body and let's race for the stars." She knew she was quickly sliding right back into the headspace she'd been in, and there was no doubt it was because they had taken the time to calm her fears and her trust had notched up to a level she'd never dreamed she could experience. She did exactly what Gage had commanded and just gave herself over to them.

They had told her they were clipping the clit clamp's chain to the one between her nipple clamps, and when Logan had told her to take a deep breath, she'd gasped as all three clamps tugged on each other. Her pussy had flooded with fresh syrup, and Gage had taken great pleasure in telling her how wonderful she tasted as he'd fucked her with his tongue. She was nearly delirious with the pleasures, and despite their demands that she hold back her release, she wasn't sure how much longer she was going to be able to obey them. She was skating on a very fine edge and was so close to a point of no return she was panting like she'd run a marathon. "Oh, please, Master Logan, Master Gage...I can't hold on much longer, it's just too much...I don't think I can do it."

"You can and you will, focus, darling. Listen carefully to my instructions and do exactly as I tell you, can you do that for us, baby?" His soft tone didn't fool her. His words weren't a request by a long shot. Seemed the good ole boy act hid a much more demanding Dom than she had ever imagined.

"Yes, Sir, I'll do exactly as you say...I, well, I want you all to be proud of me." And then she added in a soft whisper she hoped none of them heard, "I don't want to let my Master down, I love him."

Chapter 24

After Callie's near meltdown, Ian had only stepped back a few inches. He'd been determined to monitor her every breath, so he'd been close enough to hear her words. Even though he'd been sure those were the words she had held back just a few minutes before, he was still stunned at her admission. And he was even more stunned by how pleased those few words made him. Christ, he hadn't even realized how much he loved her until he'd seen the absolute trust in her eyes as he'd talked her through the fear earlier. He knew the damage her mother had done would surface again from time to time, but under his hand she'd begin to heal. Jace was already more protective of her than a pissed-off mama grizzly bear. What he wouldn't give to be a fly on the wall when Jace got to confront Chrissy Reece in a few days.

His friends had given him shit-eating grins when they'd heard Callie's words, and when they'd removed all three clamps at the same time and commanded her to come, her ear-piercing scream had covered Kalen's words behind him. "Don't fuck this up, boss. She's a keeper, and there's a long line of men, including me, who would be happy to take your place." The harshness of his words was tempered by the slap on back he gave Ian as he walked from the room.

He and Jace watched as Logan and Gage unstrapped Callie from the table and treated her nipples and tender clit with a cooling gel before they wrapped her in a soft subbie blanket and cuddled her for several minutes. Their soft words of praise were met with her sweet smile. Jace spoke up quietly, "She's amazing, thank you for allowing me to be a part of this. Capturing Callie that night on the dock was

just about the luckiest we've been in…fuck, forever. You don't plan
on letting her go, do you?"

"Never." Ian hadn't been able to take his eyes off her. She was so
amazing he couldn't believe he'd actually found a woman who could
break through the stone wall he'd built around his heart all those years
ago. "Let's take our little beauty upstairs and show her how proud we
are of her. She deserves our very best tonight." Moving forward, Ian
scooped the tiny bundle off Logan's and Gage's laps.

"Be good to her, she's earned every good thing you can give her,
boss." Logan's affection for her was obvious. After Logan had
returned home after his final mission, he'd been in a very dark place
emotionally, so seeing him connect with Callie had pleased him. Ian
was close to all the men he employed on the small island. They'd
become a community and a family of sorts—looking out for one
another and spending holidays together. Ian hoped that this was the
beginning of Logan's healing.

Jace had preceded them to the master suite and had the large tub
filling already when Ian carried Callie in and set her on her feet.
"Let's get you unwrapped and into a nice warm tub, pet. Master Jace
and I are going to get you all relaxed before we move on to your last
reward." His heart nearly caught in his throat at the look of complete
trust he saw reflected in her eyes.

"Do you need anything, sweetness? I brought you a bottle of
water, but if you're hungry I can have Inez bring you up a snack."
Jace was watching her with a careful eye, and Ian knew his friend was
almost as protective of her as he was.

"No, but thank you so much for offering…I'll be fine, and it's
late, I don't want to be a bother to Inez." Callie's words amazed Ian,
he had always been disgusted at the way the women he'd dated before
had treated his sweet housekeeper. The few who had even
acknowledged her had been disrespectful at best. Ian remembered his
father always reminding him that you could know the true measure of

someone's character by watching the way they treated their employees and the waitstaff in restaurants.

Ian reached up and stroked her cheek. "You are very sweet to consider her feelings, pet. But she honestly won't mind bringing you something if you are hungry. My guess is that she already has it prepared, because she knew some of our plans for tonight and she was concerned that you hadn't eaten much at dinner." He smiled as she automatically lowered her eyes as a pink blush washed over her sweet face.

"I was a bit nervous. And well…in that case, I would love to have a bit of a snack. Thank you." Ian watched as Jace strode from the room, eating up the distance with his long stride. No doubt he'd be back in less than a minute. Ian smiled to himself. The man was huge, but deep down he was one of the biggest teddy bears Ian knew.

* * * *

After they bathed and pampered Callie, they moved her out onto the deck. The stars were shining brightly and the weather was unseasonably warm. They'd placed candles all around, and they were going to drink a glass or two of wine while their hungry sub ate her chocolate-covered strawberries. Ian leaned back and watched as she found such joy in the simple things around her. She swore the strawberries were the best she'd ever had and that the evening was beyond perfect. She'd noticed the soft whispers of the breeze through the flower-covered vines growing up the wall and the way the lights from the shore danced across the water. She'd told them the lights looked like tiny fairies dancing on a vast stage lit by moonlight. When Ian had looked over at Jace, it was obvious he was just as captivated by her observations.

"You know, pet, you would be very good at writing the advertising for Club Isola. I'm also hoping you are interested in accepting the position as project manager for the resort." He saw her eyes go wide, and a moment later he was scrambling to refill her wine glass when she started choking. "Well, I have to say, that wasn't exactly the reaction I was hoping for, *Carlin*."

She looked up at him with tear-filled eyes, and he wasn't sure if it was from her coughing fit or from emotion. "Are you sure? You'd really want me to help you get the resort up and running? What would I do after? Oh, it doesn't really matter I guess since I'm pretty sure I'm already unemployed. Wow, I was hoping to have enough stuff left in my apartment to sell when I get back so I'd be able to get a bus ticket to my aunt and uncle's place in Kansas. But this would be better, oh so much better. Where would I work? Do you have plans drawn up already? Could I rent a room in your basement or something? I promise I'd pay you as soon as I get a check, and I could help out around here if Inez needs help. I mean, she won't want me to cook, I can promise you that, but I'm good at cleaning and organizing things. Do you think that—" She stopped in midquestion when both men burst out laughing. "What?" She tried to sound indignant rather than defensive, but she wasn't sure she'd succeeded.

Jace was the first to recover enough to respond. "Holy shit, sweetness, I don't think I've ever met another person who can ask as many questions without coming up for air as you can, well maybe Kat Lamont, but she's the only one. It's amazing, really. Now, stop for just a bit and let your Master tell you exactly what he wants. Can you do that for us, sweetheart?"

Ian had to smile at her stunned expression. He hadn't really wanted to go into all of it this evening, but her poetic observations had opened a door he just hadn't been able to walk away from. Her voice was soft and filled with appreciation. "Yes, Sir. Thank you for saving me from myself...again. You and Master Logan have your work cut out for you keeping me out of trouble, you know." *No fucking doubt about it, sweet sub.*

When Callie's attention turned to him, he simply smiled at her for a few seconds, letting her settle a bit so she'd actually *hear* what he was telling her. "Callie, I do indeed want you to take the position of project manager for the resort. The plans are drawn up already, but I would be open to reviewing them with you to see if you see anything that you feel needs to be changed. I also want you to review the advertising literature for Club Isola. The picture you just painted with your words was inspired, and I'd like to see the club's advertising image go in that direction." He stopped and just let her digest what he'd said so far. When she finally smiled, he knew she'd processed and was ready for more.

"Now, as far as renting a room, absolutely not." When he saw disappointed acceptance in her expressive eyes, he wanted to kick himself for the way he'd phrased his words. "Pet, I'm sorry, that was very poorly worded on my part. Please forgive me." When she looked up in surprise, he added, "Don't look so shocked, love. Doms are people and we make mistakes, too. And good Doms who love their subs admit them and ask for forgiveness just like any other *normal* person." He smiled at her shy nod, and he knew the second she realized he'd just told her that he loved her because her eyes went as wide as saucers and she stopped breathing. "Pet, please take a breath before you pass out on me." When she'd taken a couple of deep, gulping breaths, he heard Jace's snort of laughter to their side.

"Very good, pet, now, back to the living arrangements—you won't be sleeping anywhere but right next to me, my sweet *Carlin*. You belong to me just as I belong to you. Master Jace will be our third for as long as he wants to be. You will be much too busy working and pleasing me to have much time to help Inez, but I'm sure she will appreciate any help you are able to provide. Now, as to your belongings, everything that was in your apartment is in storage in the basement of my office complex in the city. Jace coordinated that effort the day after you arrived. We were concerned about you losing what we knew was important to you, and from the moment I set eyes on you, I knew you'd never return to that awful place." He watched as tears swamped her eyes and slowly slipped over the lids to race toward her chin. "Don't cry, my precious pet, you have brought joy back into my life and I honestly didn't think I'd ever find it again. If you agree to belong to me, I'll spend the rest of my life making you glad you did."

He wasn't sure what to expect when she stood up, and his heart nearly melted when she curled up on his lap like a soft, warm kitten wanting the physical contact and reassurance that she was loved. He wrapped his arms around her and just held her for long minutes, listening as she tried to hold in the tears that just wouldn't stop falling. She finally spoke in a whisper-soft voice, "You have no idea how long I've waited for you. You were just a dream for so many years that I still can scarcely believe you are real. And to be held in your arms…well, I haven't been hugged for years…and I'd longed for this comfort." He was speechless. How had the people who were supposed to love this woman unconditionally let her down in so many ways? Looking at his friend, he could see he was also shaken by her confession.

Ian continued to hold her close for a few moments and then drew her back so that he could see her face. Using his thumbs to wipe away her tears, he said, "Pet, you are a gift straight from heaven. Tomorrow morning, we're going into the city to get you a few things, clothing, your belongings and the like. But right now, Master Jace and I want to make sweet love to you—but in truth, watching this evening's events has taken a toll and it may turn out that we fuck you into the mattress before the sweet lovemaking part." He was relieved to hear her giggle, it sounded like his words had lightened her mood, just as he'd hoped they would. "Up you go, sweet subbie, let's get you inside before you get chilled. Our plans are better served where you are warm and comfortable." He gave her a small swat and heard her hiss as he reawakened the lingering sting from her earlier punishment. He knew from past experience, she'd likely have some heavy-duty bruises for several days, and he made a mental note to make sure he was in the dressing rooms with her tomorrow so that the snoopy sales ladies typically found in high-end boutiques would be forced to keep their distance. None of them needed that type of publicity.

Putting those thoughts aside, he whispered in her ear, "I am sure you have learned your lesson about not accepting your Master's phone calls, haven't you, pet? But just as a reminder." He gave her another small pat and laughed at her yelp as she jumped right into Jace's arms. *Perfect!*

Chapter 25

Sitting at the kitchen bar watching Inez banter with Jace, Ian sipped his coffee and thought back on last night and smiled to himself. He and Jace had spent hours taking Callie to heights of pleasure he was sure she'd not forget anytime soon. There are moments in time when everything seems in universal perfect alignment and serendipity is on your side—and last night had been one of those occasions. Sinking into her wet velvet had been part ecstasy and part torture. Holding on to his control as Jace worked himself into her sweet little ass had taken herculean effort. They had managed to bring her to the brink several times before they let her ride the wave of pleasure over the edge of control and she'd taken them right along with her.

They'd lain in bed and talked for so long that both he and Jace had been ready for round two, and despite her obvious exhaustion, she'd readily agreed to what turned out to be a marathon session where she had given him a blow job that had nearly blown the top off of his head as Jace had fucked her pussy. He'd been able to tell the instant Jace had found her sweet spot because she'd screamed around his cock, and the vibrations had made him come instantly. Damn, she might be a little bit of a woman, but she was everything he'd dreamt of and more.

He heard a shuffle outside the door and looked up just in time to see Callie step around the corner. She was wearing one of his shirts with only the middle two buttons buttoned just as he'd commanded her the first night they'd met. The meaning of her gesture wasn't lost on him, her acceptance of her submission often stole his breath. He reached out a hand to her and was pleased when she showed no hesitation in moving into his arms. "You take my breath away, pet. Your sleepy expression and tousled curls make you look like the sex kitten you are." As she settled onto his lap and curled into his arms, his heart swelled with joy.

After she'd eaten, Jace had begun questioning her about her familiarity with the small handgun he'd gotten for her. Ian had laughed at Jace's shock that Callie not only knew how to fire the weapon, but that she'd also taken it completely apart and put it back together with remarkable ease. When they'd pressed, she'd finally admitted that her uncle had been worried about her when she'd first moved in with them and this was the same gun she'd first learned to shoot.

Callie had been thrilled with the bracelet he'd given her and impressed with its safety features. Ian was proud of the pretty device he and Mitch had worked so hard on. The bracelet Callie was wearing was similar to the ones that the wives at ShadowDance all wore, but with a couple of upgrades. It not only allowed him GPS access to her at all times, it also had audio capabilities. If she was ever in trouble, all she had to do was press a recessed stone and it would transmit an audio feed directly to his security control centers on the island and at his offices on the mainland.

He and Jace had laughed at her wide-eyed appraisal. "Oh, a 'Secret Spy Walkie-Talkie' in a beautiful package. Hot damn, I never got anything this cool out of Cracker Jacks. This rocks." While he'd loved her enthusiasm, he hoped like hell she didn't ever need the pretty little device.

Callie looked absolutely stunning in the feminine sundress Daph had sent over for her. They were taking the boat over, and Ian would drive them to their destinations while Jace went to the offices and retrieved her belongings so they could be taken back to the island. He'd left Kalen and Gage to monitor things on the island, and Logan was accompanying them on their shopping expedition. What Ian hadn't told Callie was that prior to her starting work, he was planning to take her to Ireland for a couple of weeks. His company jet was standing by, and they'd be leaving as soon as Jace returned.

They weren't on high alert because Grant Westmore was currently in the midst of his confirmation hearings, so everyone had been of the opinion his father would lie low, not wanting to risk any type of exposure or publicity until things were wrapped up. They were still taking precautions, and Ian couldn't shake the feeling that he was missing something as they entered the first place Daph had recommended. The place looked like a security nightmare if you asked him, lots of nooks and crannies and dressing rooms clear at the back of the damned place. But Callie's shriek of delight as they'd walked in had been enough to distract him. She'd looked at him with such wide-eyed wonder that for just a second he'd gotten a glimpse of what she must have looked like as a child and what their daughter would look like, and that thought brought him up short. He had never considered himself parent material, but suddenly the idea wasn't nearly so foreign sounding.

"This is a beautiful store, Ian, and I appreciate you bringing me here, but honestly, there isn't going to be anything here I can afford." The sadness that had replaced the joy was soul deep, and he wondered if she'd ever been able to buy something she loved without having to worry about its cost.

"Pet, do you remember the rules of this relationship? Your well-being is my responsibility—and that includes buying you clothing and any other material goods that I'm inclined to purchase. And you are supposed to *please* me, and right now it would please me greatly if you would let me worry about the financial aspects of the things I might purchase for you." He smiled at her and was rewarded with a pink blush that let him know she had understood exactly what other purchases he'd been thinking about. As the older sales clerk approached, he turned and explained the types of things he was interested in seeing Callie try on.

He'd stood at the door of the mirror-lined dressing room watching Callie try on dozens of different outfits, some he accepted, and others he rejected before she even put them on. He's always had excellent taste in women's clothing, and he was going to relish dressing his petite sub. His cock was rock hard, and his fingers itching to free her from the lacy thong and bra he'd reluctantly allowed her to wear this morning. He finally reached behind him and locked the door. The sound echoed in the small room, and he smiled when he saw her eyes widen. "Come to me, pet. I need to sink into your softness. Watching you get into and out of all this clothing has made me hard enough to pound nails."

Callie didn't hesitate to walk into his embrace, and he immediately crashed his lips over hers in a kiss that was pure need. She opened her lips immediately and plunged her tongue into his mouth, giving as good as she got. Reaching around her, he easily tore the thong from her body and tossed the remnants into the corner. "Lean back and let me get that offending garment off of you, it hides what belongs to me." When she leaned back, he snapped the front clasp of her bra apart with a jerk, sending pieces of plastic scattering across the polished wooden floors.

While kissing her with a feeling of desperate urgency that he didn't fully understand, he managed to free his raging cock. He lifted her effortlessly, and when she wrapped her legs around him, he thrust his hips up and plunged into her hot, silken depths. "Oh, my sweet pet, you were so hot and wet—so ready for my possession. You feel amazing." After he managed to regain a small fraction of his control, he turned so that her bare back met the cool glass of the mirror. He slid her knees over his elbows and set a pounding pace. "Hang on, love, this is going to be hard and fast, and I want to take you with me. Come now, my love." He crashed his mouth over hers and caught her scream of release, and within moments they were both breathless. When he pulled back and looked into her dazed eyes, he smiled. "I just might have to rethink my previous opinion of shopping. Let's get ourselves together and get out of here. I think we've left Logan out front long enough—he probably has dates lined up through next Christmas. I'll go make our purchases and arrange for them to be delivered. Come on out when you are ready."

After righting his clothing, he made his way down the short hall and to the front of the small store. Just as he'd finished his business, his phone rang and he decided to take the call from Daphne and thank her for sending them to such a great dress shop. While he was talking with her, his phone vibrated several times with incoming calls, but he was discussing an upcoming contract and that deadline was looming, so he continued speaking with Daphne until he heard his ever-efficient administrative assistant speaking with someone to the side. "What do you mean Jace can't get through, of course he can't because I'm on the phone...What? Oh shit, why didn't you say so. Ian, Callie is trouble in the dressing room." That's all he heard before the entire store erupted into utter chaos.

Ian had glanced toward the door just in time to see Logan pocket his phone and take off running toward the dressing rooms. The big man was mowing a wide path, sending garment racks and people tumbling out of his way. The sound of shattering glass filled the store and people began to panic. Many were trying to get to the front, and they were making it difficult to maneuver around them so both he and Logan could get down the narrow hall. Logan reached the door just as they heard a gunshot, and Ian was sure his heart had stopped. *No!*

* * * *

The door reopened just seconds after Ian had left the dressing room, so Callie had been sure he'd forgotten something and hadn't bothered to turn around before asking, "Did you forget something, Master?"

"Master? Oh shit, you are kinky *and* a slut? Now that's rich, isn't it? God, you are one royal pain in the ass." Callie spun around to see

Nanette Westmore standing across from her. While pretending to cover herself, Callie pressed the small button on the bracelet Ian had given her this morning. At the time she wasn't really frightened because it was obvious the woman didn't have a weapon, but he and Jace had insisted she should press the button anytime she was uncertain of her surroundings. And she sure as hell wasn't pleased to find herself face-to-face with Senator Westmore's wife.

"Mrs. Westmore, I don't know what you want, but you need to leave. I have nothing to say to you." Callie was amazed at the venom she saw in the other woman's eyes.

"You think you can just ruin everything? I have been trying to get rid of your ass for years. Do you think you were the only pussy Grant nailed and then the hussy later swore she'd said 'no'? You were just the first of his indiscretions, he really has taken after my father in that regard, you know? And that weakling husband of mine was convinced we needed to get him help, thank God my father had enough influence to shut down John's plans before they were made public. And now that he's finally lost the last of his marbles to Alzheimer's he doesn't even remember who he is half the time. That disease has been a real pain in my ass. John was an ass before and he's even worse now. If it wasn't for my father running things from behind the scenes he'd have been bounced out of the Senate ages ago."

Callie watched as the woman's eyes became almost glassy as she continued to rail at her. "Jesus Pete, I paid your whore of a mother a lot of money to get rid of you and the child you were carrying. Hell, if you were anything like that mother of yours, who knew if it was even my son's, you should have been grateful for the cash. Hell, honey, your mom screwed most of the men at the country club and probably half the women trying to fuck her way to the top. And then she had the audacity to keep coming back for more money. It was always, 'Callie needs this or Callie needs that.' Always something."

Before she could continue, Callie spoke up. "I didn't know anything about that money until just recently. And trust me I plan to address that with my mother. And for your information, there never was a pregnancy." She paused as Nanette blinked several times, trying to take in what she'd told her.

And then the woman went completely insane, grabbing the small bench and slamming it into the mirror, sending shards of glass flying in every direction. Callie had managed to cover her eyes but felt small pieces cutting her arms. When she tried to step back, she realized she was still barefoot and the glass covering the floor made it impossible for her to move.

Nanette grabbed a long piece of glass and lunged toward her. Callie jumped back and gasped at the pain spearing the bottoms of her feet. Reaching for her small purse, Callie almost had the pistol out when the woman lunged again, slicing Callie's upper arm. Callie raised the gun and warned her, "Stop or I will shoot you, Mrs. Westmore." When she saw the woman's eyes track to her chest a split second before the muscles in her legs twitched, Callie knew she was coming for her again and fired one shot directly in to the woman's upper thigh. She hadn't wanted to kill the woman, but she damned well wasn't going to stand by and be sliced and diced either. The sound of the gun in the small room was deafening, and then all Callie could hear was Nanette's screaming and the sound of wood splintering as Logan broke through the door.

Callie watched as everything unfolded in slow motion around her. Logan tackled Nanette Westmore, pushing her face down on the floor despite the glass. He had her hands secured behind her back and had rolled her over to access the bullet wound in seconds. Ian had been right behind Logan and had wrapped her in his arms and carried her from the room. Callie looked down, and when she saw her beautiful new sundress was covered in blood, she started to cry. "My dress. Master, look what she did to my new dress. I hate her. I really liked this dress." Looking up at Ian everything started to look gauzy around the edges, and she just concentrated on his surprised smile...and it was the last thing she saw before everything went black.

Chapter 26

If Ian lived to be a hundred, he would never forget the sight of Callie standing in the small room, blood running down her arms and legs, the small pistol hanging loosely from her limp fingers, and the look of vacancy in her eyes as she watched Logan tackle her assailant. She'd stood stock-still until she'd seen him, and then it was as if someone had let the air out of a balloon. Ian had rushed to her and wrapped her in his arms just as she collapsed into his embrace. When he'd picked her up, she'd dropped the small-caliber gun. Logan had checked the safety and then pocketed it immediately. With Nanette Westmore thrashing around on the floor, no one would take a chance of her getting a hold of it. Ian moved Callie out of the room, and Logan stood Mrs. Westmore up before she cut herself to ribbons—not that it wouldn't serve the psycho-bitch right.

When his cell phone vibrated again, he answered when he saw Jace's name on the screen. "Is she all right? The guys in the control center were going ape shit when we couldn't get you on the phone. Jesus Christ, they just played a bit of the tape for me. Hell, Ian, Callie got a confession from the old hag that is going to hang her old man and her husband's asses out in the breeze. Damn, your girl is incredible."

Ian was finally able to take a deep breath and smile. He couldn't ever remember a time when Jace Garrett had actually been rattled enough to babble before this moment. He was going to get a lot of mileage out of this when his sense of humor actually came completely back online. "No, she is cut up pretty badly. Is EMS on their way?

The wounds aren't life threatening, but she has lost a lot of blood and she just passed out on my lap."

Jace's words helped keep Ian grounded. "Yes, our guys called EMS. Their ETA is three minutes from now. She probably crashed when the adrenaline dropped. Did she seem okay until she saw you?"

Ian wasn't surprised to hear Jace describe her behavior so accurately, the man had seen a lot during his years in the Special Forces. "Yes, it looked like someone had let the air out of her—she just wilted." And there was a small part of him that had wanted to beat his fists against his chest that his woman had trusted him enough to wait until he held her safely in his arms before letting go. "Call Daph, I know she is probably tearing up the office worrying about us."

"Jace just tapped me in to the call, boss. Holy flippin' hell, the press is already calling. Damn, I want a raise I tell you. I'm going to need it for hair color because mine is going to be snow white by morning." Ian chuckled, God he loved Daphne, she was the one of the best things in his life and she'd damned well get her raise. No doubt she'd earn it and more today.

"Daph, get the Lamonts on the phone ASAP and update them. Hell, with Grayson's contacts they probably already know about what's happened. Also get our guys on securing copies of that tape— lots of copies. I don't want to take any chance of losing it. Send one to Mitch for analysis. And make sure the media refers to Callie as my fiancée—and make it clear to them that anybody who trashes her paints a huge target on their own backs. Am I making myself clear?"

"Crystal…and boss? I like her. Any woman who can break down those ice blocks you've been living behind all these years has got to be one hell of a girl. I can't wait to meet her in person. If that's it, I've got work to do." She waited a half a second for his reply and then was gone with a click.

Ian felt like his entire body was going numb, and he was grateful when Jace spoke up again. "Boss, I'm walking in the front door, and as soon as I fight my way back there I'll find you." Ian hadn't even had a chance to answer before he was hung up on again by someone he was paying. *What the hell is that about anyway? Fuck, I must be getting soft.* He hadn't even finished his thoughts when Jace pushed through the doorway and crouched down in front of him and started stroking Callie's cheek. "Fuck, she looks so pale and so fragile. I swear I'd take that Westmore bitch's head off, but I want her to suffer."

When the paramedics entered the room, they'd quickly taken charge of Callie's care, and as reluctant as Ian was to hand her over, he knew she needed medical care and she'd get it much faster if he let the men do their jobs. Looking up at Jace, he simply said, "Hospital?"

Jace smiled and said, "Daph's way ahead of you. She's got the best plastic surgeon in DC waiting in the emergency room for Callie. And there will be a change of clothes for you by the time we get there. It's amazing—it's taking her longer to get the clothes there than it did for her to get a hot-shot surgeon to agree to be standing down by the back door with his thumb up his ass just waiting on your woman to arrive. I'm telling you the woman is a fucking warrior, and I swear if she wasn't old enough to be my mother I'd marry her."

Three hours later, Ian was still pacing the small private waiting room he'd been shown to when the media had swarmed the public waiting room. It still amazed him that the first question he'd been asked was if they'd set a wedding date yet. Seriously? What on earth was wrong with reporters these days? They were more interested in the society pages scooping each other with the details of Ian McGregor finally being "off the market" and that had set his teeth completely on edge. *Talk about feeling like a piece of meat!*

Once Daphne had arrived, she'd been able to run interference and manage the media while he and Jace concentrated on pacing ruts in the floor. Daph had brought along the new assistant she'd hired out of one of the other offices last week. Ian had only seen the young woman once, but considering the way she was keeping up with Daph, it looked like Holly Mills was going to be a good fit. It also looked like she had caught his best friend's eye as well, albeit for an entirely different reason.

At one point, Jace, Holly, and Daphne had all been tied up with visitors, and Ian had excused himself to a small closet down the hall. *Really classy, McGregor, fucking billions in assets and you're using a broom closet as an office. Nice.* He'd called a friend who was one of the best jewelers in the world and explained exactly what he had in mind for Callie. The man had been thrilled to hear he'd found a woman and promised to have designs e-mailed by midnight. This was one of those times that having friends was more important than money.

He walked back into the waiting room just as the doctor arrived. After explaining the extent of her injuries and all the precautions they'd had to take because of her allergy to certain pain medications, he'd told them that despite his best efforts, Callie was going to have some scarring on her upper arm, but everything else would likely heal without a trace. The doctor said that scars were problematic for people for a variety of reasons, some people were self-conscious of the way they looked and the attention they brought, citing the general public's insensitivity and incredible snoopiness. But to others, the scars were a constant reminder of a traumatic event. He'd cautioned Ian not only about making too much of an issue of the scars, but also about making too light of them also. Ian had asked the doctor to show him specifically where the scar would be, and then he'd sent a quick text message to the jeweler along with the new information.

Walking into Callie's hospital room, Ian looked down at her and wondered how such a little slip of a woman had taken over his heart without even knowing she'd done it. God, he was proud of her for remembering to activate the panic alarm and audio on her bracelet. Her quick thinking had just bought her freedom from the Westmores and was also going to bring about some long-overdue justice to a family that had had believed itself above the rules others had to abide.

When she opened her eyes and looked at him with her violet eyes awash in tears, he took her hand in his and kissed her palm. Her hand was too cold—God, she'd lost a lot of blood. That damned cut on her arm had been so deep the doctors had said she'd need physical therapy to regain her muscle strength. Her whispered "I'm sorry" brought him back to the moment.

"Pet, what do you think you have to be sorry for?" She'd been beaten down for so long that it was obvious she felt she was responsible for anything bad that happened around her. Honest to God, if he ever got his hands on her mother he wouldn't responsible for his actions. Forcing himself to relax before she picked up on his rage, he reminded himself that he was going to have a lifetime to rebuild her self-esteem.

"I know this has to be causing a media firestorm, and I didn't want to cause you that kind of trouble. I'm sure the press will have a field day with your association with me." Her tears finally breached the rim of her sad eyes and rolled down her pale cheeks. He brushed them away with his thumbs and swallowed past the lump that had formed in his throat.

"Well, I have wonderful staff that are happily telling anyone with a press card who will listen how my brave fiancée was attacked by the crazed wife of a senator. And how my woman's quick thinking led to the arrest of not only the wife, but also her husband." He smiled at her shocked expression—he wasn't sure if it was his use of the word fiancée or the news that the Westmores had been arrested. "Now, they probably won't be convicted, but the arrest along with Nanette's attack on you will leave their reputations in tatters. And now that the news of his physical condition is out, he'll be relieved of his Senate seat immediately. As for me not wanting to be associated with you, you couldn't be any more wrong."

Just then Daph knocked quietly and then stuck her head in the door. "Ian, I have a call on the line I believe you'll want to deal with personally." Her sly smile let Ian know his cagey admin was up to some sort of no good, and he had a sneaking suspicion he was going to enjoy it. "I'd be happy to stay with Callie while you take this out in the hall." Oh yeah, she was up to something all right. *Very smooth, Daph, very smooth indeed.*

He took the phone from her and moved past her into the hall before raising it to his ear. "This is Ian McGregor." He knew his words sounded curt, but he didn't care.

"Oh, Mr. McGregor, this is Chrissy Reece, and I just heard on the news about you and my sister…and well, how she was injured and all, so I wanted to check and see how she was." Oh he'd just bet the fact she had noted her sister's relationship with him before inquiring about her well-being was the mother of all Freudian slips. "You know, Callie and I are so very close. She'd helped me a lot over the years."

"Yes, Ms. Reece, I'm fully aware of how much you have relied on your sister for the past several years. As to your inquiry about her health, she will be fine. She was cut by a shattered mirror, but she should be dismissed from the hospital in a few hours. After that she'll be back in my care. If you have any further questions for her, I'll be happy to pass along your concerns, and she can call you when she is feeling stronger." Ian was one of the most influential businessmen in the country, so dealing with venomous people was an everyday occurrence, but this woman obviously brought out the very worst in him. Her treatment of Callie over the years galled him, and it was going to stop right now.

"Well, I am perfectly happy to speak with you, Ian, you don't mind that I call you by your first name, do you? I mean, after all, we're going to be family." She practically purred, and Ian was getting angrier by the second.

She was still rambling on when Ian interrupted her, "Ms. Reece, I want to make my position here perfectly clear. I am in love with your sister. And a part of that, a very large part in fact, is my commitment to care for her and protect her from potential harm." He paused for just a few seconds to give her a chance to catch on, if that was possible, before he continued. "Any potential or real threats to her health or happiness will be dealt with swiftly and decisively. Do I make myself clear?"

"Well, you know I'd never do anything to hurt my sister, Ian. Perhaps I'll just drive up and visit her. Yes, that sounds like a wonderful idea." She hadn't really listened to a word he said. And why that surprised him was anybody's guess.

"We'll be leaving on a trip in a day or two. So perhaps you could wait until we've returned. Callie needs to rest, and then we'll be out of the country for a short time. I'll have her call you as soon as we return. Thank you for calling. Good day, Ms. Reece." He hung up before he screamed what a selfish piece of trash he considered her.

He walked back in the room to find his assistant and Callie talking and laughing like old friends. It was easy to see why her coworkers spoke so highly of her, she had a natural way of speaking with people that seemed to draw them out. "Well, I see you two seem to have hit it off nicely. Daph, where the hell is that doctor with Callie's paperwork? Christ, these people won't ever get anything done if we don't push them." He'd no sooner spoken than the two women looked at each other and burst out laughing.

As Daphne made her way toward the door, she looked at him and said, "On it, boss." And then looked at Callie and added, "Welcome to my world, Callie. I'll be seeing you soon. It was a pleasure to finally meet you. Oh…and good luck, dear." And then laughing at Ian's snarl, she was gone.

Chapter 27

Six Months Later

Callie stood in the shadows in the Main Lounge at Club Isola watching as her new friends moved around the room engaging in animated conversations and enjoying the celebratory atmosphere of the evening. Although the room still looked like it belonged in a European castle, it had been transformed so that it more closely resembled a ballroom and banquet hall than a torture chamber. Most of the BDSM equipment had been moved against the walls that were now draped in hundreds of yards of silver-gray gossamer.

She knew there were over twelve hundred flameless candles lighting the room. *Oh yeah, the Energizer Bunny is alive and well on the island tonight.* She had been so busy overseeing the resort's construction that she hadn't been that involved in the planning for this evening's celebration. Only a very select few people knew that she and Ian had wed this evening at sunset on the private beach below their home. Sometimes she still struggled to grasp the changes her life had undergone in the past six months.

Glancing down at the beautiful ring Ian had given her, she smiled as the candle's flickering lights danced over all the facets of the enormous, radiant cut diamond. She loved the woven band because it reminded her of all the beautiful Celtic knots and their meanings she'd learned about while touring Ireland with Ian and Jace after the nightmare at the dress shop. She hadn't realized Jace had stepped up beside her until he spoke. "Nervous, Mrs. McGregor?" Jace was to be her official "escort" until the collaring ceremony.

She noticed that he'd changed from his earlier tux and that he was now dressed in black dress trousers and a black silk shirt that was open several more buttons than you'd expect to see at most formal occasions. *Lord, you have to love the kink community. They take a formal occasion and add their own twist, and the men end up looking more yummy than the women. Well, duh, Callie, that's because most of the women are not wearing all that much.* Smiling to herself she turned and answered. "Yes, very. I haven't done anything public since that first disaster…and well…I am worried that I'll mess up…again." She looked up at him through her lashes, worried she'd see pity, but all she saw was understanding.

"Sweetness, you didn't mess up. You used your safe word, and that is exactly what a sub is supposed to do when things are too much either physically *or* emotionally." When she shivered at the memory of that night, he looked at her thoughtfully and added, "Are you cold?"

Knowing he'd seen her absently rubbing her hands up and down her upper arms, she deliberately tried to still the movement. It had become a habit more because she was so self-conscious of the large scar on her arm than anything else. "No, I'm fine. Has Ian come down from his office yet? I haven't seen my new husband yet."

Jace chuckled. "Worried I'm going to tie you up on the stage and leave you naked for all to see and he isn't gonna show, sweetness?"

Callie felt her face go instantly hot and knew she had flushed bright red. "Well, something like that, yeah. I mean, that would be pretty embarrassing, and I'm already worried about how much my scar is going to show up under the lights." She saw him frown so she quickly added, "Yes, I know, I'm not supposed to worry, that I am only supposed to submit and leave the worries to Ian…and you." She smiled at him sweetly and gave him a quick hug.

"Good save, sweetness." He laughed and pulled her tighter against his chest. "Just so you'll stop worrying yourself into a tizzy—Ian is out at the dock greeting some very special guests. He'll be here any minute. And as for how you'll be dressed, well, I think I'll let you fret on that one for a bit longer." He laughed out loud and leaned down and kissed the top of her head before he released her from his embrace. Nodding toward the door, he said, "Looks like they have arrived. Ian will seat them while I take you to the stage. Come on, let's get this show on the road, shall we?"

The butterflies that had been fluttering around in her stomach suddenly turned into B-51 bombers hell bent on mass destruction. She must have gone pale because Jace suddenly had his arm around her waist, and she was grateful when she stumbled and nearly took a header off the small step she where she'd been standing. Jace turned her so that she was facing him and tilted her face up so that he was the only thing she could see. The lights in the large room had been dimmed, and the soft stage lighting was enough to illuminate his face so she could see his protective expression.

"Sweetness, have I ever lied to you?" He waited patiently for her reply.

She was light headed, and all she could think about was that there were now important people in the audience and how horrible it was going to be if she let Ian down. She loved him with everything in her, and failure was just not an option.

Jace gave her a swat on the ass and snarled. "Sweetness, I asked you a question."

His tone brought her back to the moment, "No, Sir, you have never lied to me, I trust you…as I trust my Master."

"Very good, sweetness. Now, know this, your Master and I are both very possessive bastards, and we didn't much like sharing you all those months ago. And you may be married to Master Ian, but I am still your permanent third. And, sweetness, that means I have some very strong feelings about how this evening should go." He smiled when her eyes went wide. He stroked his finger down her cheek, and the calming effect that simple move had was amazing. His words changed to a sweet whisper. "Callie, Ian and I are both well aware of how self-conscious you are about the scar. Trust us." He waited for her nod, and then he turned and led her up the steps to the stage.

* * * *

After Ian had seated his friends, he'd turned to see Callie stumble, and he'd watched as Jace had steadied her. Just as he'd started to head that way, Mitch Grayson had reached out and stopped him. "Jace is handling it, she is just scared she's going to let you down and she's worried about that fucking scar on her arm. What is it with women and scars? Christ, Rissa freaks out about her C-section scar, and God knows that's not nearly as visible as Kat's whiplashes." Ian knew his friend had kept talking long enough to let Jace speak with Callie without his interference, and he was grateful. He knew it was important to Callie that she do well tonight. He wanted her to succeed more for her own self-confidence in the lifestyle than for him.

He had known the scar on her arm was going to be a huge reminder of all she'd endured, and he watched on their trip as she had repeatedly tried to dress in clothing that had long enough sleeves to cover up the indelible proof of Nanette Westmore's insanity. Hopefully, after tonight, she'd feel she had a reason to show off those beautiful, long, slender arms of hers. Her social position as his wife and her job at the resort would require her to wear ball gowns often, and he wanted her to feel as beautiful and elegant as she was. He knew as well as anyone, self-confidence shines from within.

Taking a last look around the table where his friends had gathered, he was humbled by the fact that so many of the ShadowDance Mountain crew had flown in for tonight's collaring. They had teased him, saying they were only coming so they could meet the woman who'd shot a senator's wife, but he knew the women had come as a show of support for a fellow sub and "warrior chick," as Kat Lamont had so eloquently stated.

Ian moved to the edge of the stage where he would be shadowed, but he knew his new bride would know he was close. He smiled to himself as she immediately seemed to settle. *That's right, my love, you are mine...your heart, your soul, and your future are all safely in my care.*

The dress she wore was perfect for what he had planned. It was strapless but tightly fitted so the zipper in the back would allow them to lower it just enough for this scene. He knew he was going to be pushing the boundary of his own club charter to the point it might snap under the strain. But he'd informed all the staff anyone with a problem with how things played out this evening was to be sent directly to him. And those that really kicked up a fuss would have their pro-rated membership fees refunded and would be out—permanently. It was simple as far as he was concerned—His wife—His club—His rules.

When Jace had Callie secured to the St. Andrew's cross, he took the small headset from the assistant and walked on to the small stage. Walking around so that he faced Callie, he smiled down in to her soft expression. "You are so very beautiful, and you are mine—*forever*. But I also belong to you, my love, never forget that. Now, let's play a bit shall we?" He knew she'd understand that by using the word *play* he was sending her a very clear message. *Yes, my love, this is not going to be what all those nasty little brat subs have been filling your head with for the past several weeks. You're going to fly right over the moon and love every minute of it.*

He turned on his headset and addressed their audience even as he kept his palm along her face. "Good evening, everyone, and thank you for joining us for this very special occasion." He leaned forward and kissed her on the forehead and then moved around to face everyone. "As you know, members who choose to have us host their collaring ceremony are bound by certain guidelines." He chuckled and then continued, "I assure you I'm going to meet each of those in spirit, if not be their strictest interpretation."

Pausing for a few seconds, he nodded to Jace, who moved to the cabinet and withdrew the long bullwhip they'd be using. "Now, what most of you do not know is that Callie and I were married earlier this evening on the beach as the sun set over the bay. It was absolutely perfect in every way." The entire room erupted in applause and shouts of congratulations. He smiled at her in the mirrors and enjoyed the flush of embarrassment that the response had caused. "Now, that being said, we are going to continue with the collaring, but I'll be giving my beautiful wife two lashes with a bullwhip as a pledge that our two hearts shall always beat as one. Master Jace will give her one as a pledge to love and protect her as our third."

He wanted to get this done as quickly as possible because he could hear her breathing speeding up already. *Don't panic, baby, don't go there.* Ian was relieved to see that Jace had already unzipped and lowered her dress so that her beautiful bare back and ass were displayed before him. While he warmed up his arm, he watched as Jace stepped in front of Callie and began seducing her right up to the edge of release. He planned to pull the lashes and would need every bit of concentration, so he quickly tuned out Jace's words to her.

* * * *

Jace had watched Callie carefully and knew that the moment she'd heard the words *bull* and *whip* she had nearly screamed her safe word. He was glad he'd decided to stand in front of her because he couldn't every remember seeing her looking so frightened and vulnerable. *Christ, she wasn't this pale in the hospital.*

"Callie, I asked you a question." Jace's stern tone brought her attention back to him.

"Oh, Master Jace, I'm sorry, I was sort of…well, lost for a moment. Can you repeat it please?" Her voice was too tight and high, he needed to get her back under his control and quickly. He had no intention of letting either of his friends down.

"I asked you if you trusted us, sweetness. Don't fall into panic. Show us how much you trust us to do exactly what is best for you." Just as he'd spoken, Ian landed the first of his two lashes. Jace watched as her eyes went wide, and he knew it would have felt like a quick line of fire down her back—startling, but far from the pain she had been expecting. He pinched her peaked nipples and then rolled them tightly between his fingers and heard her moan softly. She fell into the sensations quickly, and he was pleased when she arched her back after Ian's second lash. He knew they were pulling the lashes because Ian didn't want this to be how she remembered her wedding night, and he had agreed. He leaned forward and kissed her lightly before moving off to the side so that Ian could take his place.

As he walked around a movement at the side of the crowd caught his eye despite the bright stage lights. Taking the whip from the assistant, he realized the woman he'd seen was Holly Mills, the voluptuous beauty that had been working in Ian's downtown executive offices for the past year or so. A couple of months ago he'd walked around the corner outside the office building and seen Holly stumble back from out of a man's reach. He was sure the man had been yelling before he'd seen Jace, but when he'd stopped to check on Holly, she had insisted she was all right. She had missed the next several days of work, and Daph had said she had called in with the flu. He hadn't believed it, but hadn't had a chance to make any further inquiries. Leaning down, he instructed the sub who was working as the stage assistant to find Master Gage immediately. If Holly was here because she was interested in the lifestyle, the evening had just gotten a lot more interesting.

Turning back to Callie, he walked up and slowly traced Ian's lash marks with the pads of his fingers. He planned to lay his alongside the others. He and Ian had everything timed out, and she was right where they wanted her to be. Leaning forward, he licked the shell of her ear and whispered, "When my lash falls, you will come for us. Scream your Master's name so that the entire world knows that your heart and soul belong to Ian." He bit the lobe and moved back at her moan.

His lash landed perfectly, and the instant the line streaked down her beautiful back she came, screaming Ian's name. Jace was pleased to see everyone in the audience had stayed quiet in respectful silence waiting for Callie to be released and to kneel at Ian's feet to receive her collar. Ian hadn't wanted her to be naked as was the tradition, so as he was releasing her arms while Jace raised and secured her beautiful violet gown.

Chapter 28

Ian turned her and once again addressed the audience. "My beautiful wife has pleased me in more ways than I can tell you. Her beauty radiates from her soul all the way to the surface and shines so that it warms everyone around her. Because she is so extraordinarily special, I have chosen something unique to show the world that she belongs to me. I wanted something that leaves no doubt that Callie McGregor is the most important person in my life." Jace had picked up the velvet box from the side cabinet and opened it for him. He saw Callie's unfocused gaze land upon the contents.

Ian had worked closely with the designer making sure her beautiful ring, the arm bracelet, and matching ankle bracelet were perfect in every way. The Celtic designs reflected his Irish heritage and were also reminiscent of their trip to Ireland months ago. The McGregor family crest was stamped in the design as were the words "Ian's Carlin." The arm piece would effectively camouflage the scar that Callie was so self-conscious of as well. The pieces were magnificent. Literally, one-of-a-kind masterpieces that would likely be featured in every fashion magazine for weeks—along with speculation as to what the unique jewelry represented. *Let them wonder.*

Ian saw Jace whisper to Gage and the other man glance to the side of the room and then nod. Following their line of sight, Ian had to smile to himself. He knew who Gage had just been sent to secure, and he was glad Jace was finally going to make a move on the woman who had caught his eye so many months ago.

Looking back at Callie, he saw her eyes widened with appreciation and love and then filled to overflowing with her sweet tears. "Callie, by accepting these gifts, you are acknowledging me as your Dom, your protector, your mentor and provider, and your lover. I want to remind you that as my submissive, you will follow my orders, keep no secrets, and you will trust that every decision I make is made with my love and commitment to you in mind. You own my heart, my love." Ian slid both bands into place before snicking the hidden locks closed.

"Yes, Master." She kissed the small titanium key he held to her lips, and then he dropped the chain holding the small octagon shaped key back inside his shirt. Smiling to himself, Ian thought about all the hours he and Jace had spent designing the hidden locks and the look of fascination on the young jeweler's face as they'd explained the drawings to him. Ian had given each man one half of the royalties off the design they had patented. He'd lend his name and the Club Isola endorsement so the lock would probably be worth millions to each of them for several years to come. His only request had been that the young jeweler break the molds for Callie's pieces.

As they'd planned, Jace stepped to the front of the stage and spoke to the applauding group. "Ian and Callie will be taking a few minutes to themselves, and then they are hoping to greet each and every one of you at the reception. In the meantime, the bar is now open, the food has been set out, and it's time to celebrate. Here's to a very special union, good friends, and future celebrations filled with whips, chains, leather, and lace." Ian had laughed out loud at his friend's boisterous start to a party that would certainly last until dawn's first light...but first, he had a newly collared bride to attend to.

THE END

WWW.AVERYGALEBOOKS.COM

ABOUT THE AUTHOR

For years, I was accused of living in my own little "Fantasy Land" so I decided to put it to use and started writing. I enjoy creating characters who are loveable but never perfect, who live in and visit places I'd love to go, and who overcome obstacles to find the sexy happily ever after I believe we all deserve. I fall in love with the characters I create and enjoy making them each wacky and wonderful in their own way.

The only consistent trait in my heroines is their inability to cook and that is the only trait they each have "inherited" from me. When I'm not working at my very ordinary job, I am either writing or reading. And even though my family professes to support my writing efforts, but I'm fairly certain they are merely glad to see I've finally found an outlet for what they have always considered my over-the-top imagination.

For all titles by Avery Gale, please visit
www.bookstrand.com/avery-gale

Siren Publishing, Inc.
www.SirenPublishing.com

Lightning Source UK Ltd.
Milton Keynes UK
UKOW032152260613

212876UK00021B/2072/P

9 781627 401531